KILLER MEMO

STELLA KNOX SERIES: BOOK FIVE

MARY STONE
STACY O'HARE

Copyright © 2022 by Mary Stone

All rights reserved.

No part of this book may be reproduced in any form or by any electronic or mechanical means, including information storage and retrieval systems, without written permission from the author, except for the use of brief quotations in a book review.

❦ Created with Vellum

DESCRIPTION

When death leaves a warning...

FBI Special Agent Stella Knox hasn't finished the paperwork on her last assignment when she walks straight into her next case. A memo written on bright yellow paper looks unassuming at first.

What are you afraid of, Paul Slade?

It's a curious question. One the Special Agent in Charge of the Nashville office doesn't take seriously...at first.

One note might have been a joke. Two were a plan. A third leads to a missing deputy. And when a fire inspector mysteriously vanishes, it's clear someone is deliberately targeting the city's most courageous city servants—and wants them to know it.

As Stella and her team scramble to pinpoint who's behind the disappearances, a killer is playing a deadly game of cat and mouse...and the FBI office is next.

Suspenseful and unnerving, Killer Memo is the fifth book in the Stella Knox Series by bestselling author Mary Stone and Stacy O'Hare. Are you ready to face your worst fear? Too bad if you aren't.

1

What the hell was I thinking?

Darkness and boredom surrounded Deputy Carlos Guerrero, causing him to ponder the majority of his life choices. Especially his most recent one.

A few hours ago, setting a speed trap at the highway exit had seemed like an excellent idea. After all, the potential for catching drunk drivers along this stretch was pretty darn good. Hell, he'd even been excited at the prospect of pressing the pedal to the metal in order to stop a muscle car or crotch rocket from using the smooth stretch of concrete as a racetrack.

He'd been wrong.

Not a single soul was out this early in the morning, and he was bored to tears.

Carlos lifted his coffee cup, noticed it was empty for the third time in twenty minutes, and dropped it back into its holder.

The only light was the glow of his onboard computer, and it was so bright it hurt his eyes.

"Almost done, man. Almost done." The sound of his own

voice didn't do much to keep him alert. Of course, *almost done* wasn't the perkiest pep talk, but for the life of him, he couldn't think of anything more exciting to say.

With a groan, he picked up his phone and texted Maria.

Almost done. Home soon.

Figuring stretching his legs would do him good, he opened the door and stepped out into the inky black of the quiet Tennessee night. He'd take a few breaths of the sweet summer air, climb back into his cruiser, and mosey on back to the station.

His eyes took longer than normal to adjust to the deep darkness before the dawn, with afterimages of the computer screen creating bluish imprints against the horizon. The sky brightened as two beams of light approached. Rather than exiting the highway, though, the rocky roll of wheels pulling up behind him broke through the otherwise soft sounds of the outdoors.

Deputy Guerrero turned.

A truck—maybe a brown or rusty red GMC—parked a few feet behind the cruiser's rear bumper. Dull headlights, with bulbs that needed changing, seemed to cast more shadows than they cut through. They were aimed right at Carlos's face and forced him to raise a hand to shade his eyes.

The door to the truck opened, and a deep voice broke the silence. "Sorry, Deputy. I'm almost out of gas and I don't think I can make it to the next station. Thought you might have a gallon?"

Finally, something to do. Good Samaritan time.

"Sure thing." Carlos hit the button on his key fob and popped the trunk. "Everything else okay?"

"Oh, yes, sir. Everything else is just fine. Just feeling kinda dumb. Here, let me help you."

The driver climbed out of the cab. He was all shadow and muscle. The man was a few inches taller than Carlos, but other details of his features were hard to determine in the current lighting. They met at the open trunk.

Carlos kept his sidearm away from the motorist. *Can't be too careful.*

"Where you headed?" He lifted a red emergency kit to reveal the gas can.

"Almost home." The driver took the can.

Carlos dropped the emergency kit back into the trunk.

"Just a few miles to go."

"Almost safe and sound." Carlos slammed the trunk shut.

"Aren't you afraid out here? In the dark? I mean, anyone could just show up."

It wasn't the first time Carlos had been asked that question. "I'm not afraid of the dark. Same stuff is in the dark that's in the light."

The man chuckled. He took a few steps back to his truck, hefting the thirty-pound can around as if it weighed next to nothing. "So what *are* you afraid of?"

Before the deputy could fully process the question, the man swung. The container connected with the side of Carlos's head. His skull exploded, shards of pain radiating from his ear and down his neck in sharp crackles as his knees buckled and gravel rushed up to greet him.

The night burst into a flashing ball of orange and gold from the impact. But the colors were all in Carlos's head, blurring together. As if from a distance, he watched the gas can coming toward his face, but he couldn't even lift his hands.

A second later, all the colors blinked out.

WHEN HE CAME TO, Carlos wasn't sure where the pain was coming from. His back screamed. His head thumped as though someone was beating on the inside of his skull with a couple of steel hammers. A siren hummed in his right ear. But even those agonies were nothing compared to the ache pulsing down his neck, across his shoulders, and through his arms. Pain throbbed through his body from the inside out.

He tried to move, to at least cover his ears to block the mind-bending noise, but he couldn't. For a wild moment, he thought he was paralyzed, until it registered that his hands were bound behind his back. Kicking his feet, he realized they were also tied. Looking down, he saw layer upon layer of duct tape wound around his ankles.

Trying to understand his situation, he glanced around as much as his stiff neck would allow. He was curled inside some kind of crate. The wooden walls held him so close, he couldn't roll fully onto his back. The most he could do was lean a little, a move that eased the strain in his shoulders but squashed his fingers against the bottom of his compact prison.

Carlos's dark blue uniform shirt had come untucked from his trousers, leaving patches of skin exposed to the rough wood. A splinter dug into his upper hip.

Worse, his duty belt was missing, meaning his flashlight, pepper spray, and gun were all gone. The radio, normally attached to his shoulder, was no longer a head twist away, and his phone wasn't in his pocket.

What's happening?

Flashes of a truck with dull headlights came to mind. A man asking for help. A gas can. The heavy weight slamming into his head.

Dammit.

He'd been off his game from the boredom, from the late hour, and from manning his shift alone once again. Ezra Forman, his partner, had been pulled for a different time slot.

The short staffing was nearing unsustainable levels. Couldn't even put two partners together for an everyday traffic roster.

Carlos tried to turn a little more and winced as splinters on the crate's wall scraped against his arm. He leaned away from the wall as much as he could, and blood rushed back into his fingertips. The ache in his right shoulder deepened.

Don't feel, dammit. Think.

The pain in his head was his only response. But between the dull pulses throbbing behind his eyelids, he remembered...

Tall. Muscular. Strong.

What else? The guy had lifted the gas can and swung it like it weighed nothing. Carlos's head could testify that it weighed significantly more than *nothing*.

"What are you afraid of?" That's what the man had asked.

Who is this guy? Carlos couldn't come up with an immediate answer. Who would kidnap a deputy and throw him into a crate? Scenarios of human trafficking, kidnap-for-ransom, and torture burned through his brain.

But him? Why?

Dazed as he was, he couldn't get a clear motive in his pounding head.

Angry and frustrated now, Carlos twisted his wrists, trying to loosen his bonds with new fervor. When he got hold of whoever did this... *Man, there wouldn't be a hole deep enough to throw the bastard in.* Assaulting a deputy would be but the first in a long list of charges.

That asshole was going to trip on so many stairs after Carlos brought him in, he'd get PTSD just *looking* at a stepladder.

He paused in his attempts to wriggle loose. Listened.

Silence. Emptiness. No one was there. He let his shoulder fall back against the side of the crate. Numbness returned to his fingers. With his shoulder supporting him, at least the splinter in his back wasn't pressing any deeper.

His eyes adjusted to the gloom. The box wasn't completely dark. Narrow gaps between the four-inch planks let in thin lines of yellow light. The dim glow highlighted the crate's rough, unplaned walls that were secured together by old, rusty nails. And he saw something else.

A black spider, which sat in the center of its web above Carlos's thigh.

It was huge, at least a couple of inches if it spread itself out. The shafts of yellow light cast the spider's shadow against the wood. It seemed larger than his knee. Thin, wicked legs maneuvered against the web. Carlos's chest tightened as revulsion and fear punched him in the gut. His breath came in short, fast gasps. The ringing in his ears grew louder.

It's just a spider, man. Just a bug. You've got bigger things to worry about than a damn arachnid.

The spider sat there, shifting from one thread to another. Watching him with little spider eyes...

Eight years old. He climbed into bed and slipped his legs under the blanket. So warm, so welcoming...until the short, sharp stab on the back of his calf jarred him awake. He whipped down the blanket just in time to watch the brown spider run across the sheet and disappear under the mattress.

He'd only seen the spider for a second. It wasn't big or especially ugly. He was sure it wasn't one of those venomous creatures that could kill a man. The bite was from just a regular house spider, no bigger than his thumbnail.

But the reaction started an instant later.

The bite swelled and grew hot and itchy. His lips ballooned, and his throat tightened. He struggled to breathe as he stumbled downstairs to the living room.

Carlos's mom and dad drove him to the emergency room, where he received an injection with a needle as long as his arm.

"You could have died, hijo."

That's what they told him. And ever since then, before he got into bed, he'd pull down the blanket to check that there were no spiders hiding between the sheets.

And now, a spider, a damn big one, was his crate mate.

"Hey!" Fear caused the word to warble. "Get me outta this damn box."

Silence.

The web rippled as the spider lifted one leg, then another. Though Carlos hadn't dared move, the damn thing jolted forward as if it'd been poked by a prod. It scurried onto the planking. As he watched in numb horror, it made its way across the top of the box until it was directly over the zipper of Carlos's trousers. Goose bumps formed on the skin exposed by his untucked shirt.

"God. No. Get out of here. Go on."

There were gaps between the planks, plenty of places for the hairy beast to escape through. Surely, it would leave. It would scurry through the space and leave him alone. Spiders didn't like people. That's what his mom always said.

But it didn't leave. With a jerk, the spider lowered itself until it hung a couple of inches from his body. There wasn't even a breeze to blow the critter's legs back to the wall.

"No, no." Carlos sucked in his belly button. "Please no."

As if the web had been cut, the spider fell onto the waistband of Carlos's pants.

Carlos froze. If he moved, the spider would jump onto his belly and sink its fangs into his skin. He was sure it would. And then he'd suffocate in there. His throat would close, he'd struggle to breathe, and he'd die. Venom from a pesky bug was going to accomplish what a dozen years of criminals, drunks, and angry drivers hadn't managed to do.

The spider turned. It paused for a moment on Carlos's trouser button, then slowly made its way up over his waistband, one leg, then another, then another, onto the bare skin of his belly.

Carlos tried not to shudder. He held his breath. The spider's sharp little legs tickled his skin. How he wanted to jump up, twist his torso, and scratch his stomach until he'd removed the top layer of skin.

He exhaled carefully, keeping perfectly still.

Get a grip. It's just a damn spider. You're a cop. You've handled worse than this.

He just needed to control his fear response, control his breathing.

In and out. That's it. That thing's not biting. Just stay still.

The tickle crawled up his waist. A second later, the spider skittered up until it reached the side of Carlos's rib cage. If he moved fast…

Without giving himself time to think his actions through, Carlos rolled onto his side, forcing his ribs into the unfinished planks. Pain shot down one arm, and the splinter in his back screamed. The tip of his knee banged the side of the box.

None of that mattered when a sticky wetness spread along his side.

In the dim light, he grinned.

"Gotcha, little bastard."

Footsteps sounded outside the crate. Carlos froze in place. A deep shadow cut through the thin streams of light. He held his breath, not wanting whoever was on the other side of the planks to hear his struggles. Something about the surety of the footsteps told Carlos the man from the truck stood just outside his cage. All the muscles in his body tensed, ready to fight or roll away.

As the breath he was holding grew stale in his lungs, the

lid was thrown back, and the yellow light that had leaked through the planks filled the crate. It was just bright enough to cause Carlos's eyes to water. He blinked to clear his vision.

He was in a barn. Carlos could make out a hayloft that was so warped it looked like it was ready to collapse at any second. Rafters crisscrossed along the ceiling. Overhead, a bare lightbulb cut through the grayish light of early morning leaking in around the barn door.

A figure stood over him. The dim glow cast him into a silhouette. Carlos couldn't make out the figure's face. Again. It was like the man was made of shadow.

He could, though, make out a large box the man gripped between his fingertips.

His captor leaned over the crate. "Are you ready to answer my question?"

Carlos twisted, trying to get a better look at the man's face. "What question?"

"What are you afraid of?"

The man slid the lid off the box he held. Another spider, small and brown, sped over the man's thumb and dropped into the crate. Carlos couldn't see where it landed.

Incongruously, Carlos thought of Maria. Two nights ago, he'd leapt away from a spider in the kitchen sink. She had laughed before scooping the li'l beast up in a paper towel and setting it loose in the backyard.

Was this lunatic inside his head? Had he been stalking Carlos, watching from the kitchen window that night? A box of snakes would've been less scary. How did this guy learn about his greatest fear?

Another spider, black and orange, crawled over the top of the box and dropped into the crate.

Carlos gritted his teeth to stop a scream from escaping.

No way was he going to let this creep see how scared he

was. He held still, trying not to startle the arachnids now crawling around somewhere outside his line of vision.

"You're the one who should be scared." He tried and failed to use the command voice he'd learned in the academy. "Of what I'll do to you when I get out of here."

The man gave a short laugh. "Good. That's good. How about now?"

He upended the box. A stream of spiders—all sizes, all colors—cascaded through the air and into the crate, their legs and bodies spiraling toward Carlos in the yellow light.

The creatures filled every empty space. They clambered over Carlos's legs, his shoulders, his neck, his cheeks. And still, they kept coming. He was drowning in an endless sea of spiders.

Carlos opened his mouth to scream, and a long, hairy leg brushed his upper lip.

It touched his tongue.

As he flailed, tiny fangs sank into his skin.

His leg. His head. His face.

The lid of the crate slammed shut.

2

FBI Special Agent Stella Knox licked her lips as the scent of fresh, buttery croissants and strong brewed coffee made her mouth water and her stomach growl. Coco's, the café beneath her apartment, always smelled liked heaven in the morning.

"My usual, please. And I'll take one of these."

She lifted an enormous chocolate chip cookie from the box on the counter while Kate steamed milk for the hot chocolate Stella preferred. The cookie was the size of a small plate and contained enough chips to choke a horse.

She reached for another. "Make it two."

Kate smiled. She was a pretty twenty-something with bleached blond hair that needed a touch-up. Or maybe the dark roots were on purpose? Even at the still-youthful age of twenty-eight, Stella couldn't keep up with the ever-changing trends anymore. Not that she wanted to. No trend would keep her from pulling her long, dark strands back into the sensible ponytail she preferred.

Stella tucked the second cookie into her bag. It was for Mac, a friend and colleague who deserved a reward much bigger and more expensive than this chocolatey treat, but it would have to do for now. Special Agent Mackenzie Drake had put herself on the line to help Stella investigate the murder of her father.

Mac's snooping had led to the shocking discovery that Joel Ramirez, a man Stella thought of as "Uncle Joel," hadn't been killed in the line of duty, as was reported. He was alive and well and living in Atlanta under another name.

Stella still couldn't believe it.

Like the cyber beast she was, Mac had found the family address of her father's former partner. Following the lead, Stella and fellow agent Hagen Yates had driven down to Georgia to speak to Joel's surviving family. The hope was that Joel had told a family member some important tidbit about Stella's father's death.

To her shock and surprise, Joel himself had walked out his front door. She and Hagen had been trying to regroup from that curveball when they received the call for their last case.

She sighed. If she'd only been granted an additional few hours last weekend, she would have pulled her shit together and confronted the man who'd lied to her family for so long. She'd have learned why the trusted cop—who'd been like a second father to her—disappeared.

She could have discovered what else he knew about her father's killing too.

Because he knew something. Her gut insisted he did.

The night before he faked his own death, Uncle Joel had arrived on her porch and drunkenly claimed that dirty cops had killed her father, that Stella's dad had been betrayed by one of his own.

No! Not Uncle Joel, she reminded herself. She could no longer think of him like that. Not until she'd spoken to him face to face. Learned the truth behind his duplicity.

If she and Hagen hadn't been called to Chapel Island to crack a series of cheerleader murders, she'd have the answers to all those questions by now. Or at least some of them.

A giant chocolate chip cookie to start a Friday morning was the very least Mac deserved.

"Stella?"

She blinked and came back to the present as Kate placed the hot chocolate on the counter and rang up her items. Under different circumstances, Stella might have been embarrassed to be caught daydreaming. But Kate had seen Stella space out before and never seemed to judge. And she knew how to make her hot chocolate exactly the way she liked it, light on the chocolate and with extra frothy cream.

"Sorry. Miles away."

She paid, dropping an extra couple of bucks in the tip jar. That should prevent Kate from gossiping too hard about the absent-minded FBI agent from upstairs.

Stella gathered her goodies and headed to her 4Runner. She'd save her own cookie for the office. She savored the warm drink as she drove, using its sweetness to ease into the day...and to knock out the bitterness of the previous evening, another topic she wanted to discuss with Mac.

Last night had started so well. After solving the cheerleader murder case, she'd wanted nothing more than a meal and her bed. Hagen's unexpected offer to come over with bags of Korean takeout had made Stella think *this* would be the moment. He'd open up and tell her about the death of his own father. He'd discuss how he felt now, and he'd explain the real reason he wanted to help her confront Joel Ramirez.

Even after working with Hagen Yates for a few weeks now, Stella still wasn't sure what made the man tick. He could have come with her to Atlanta last weekend because he genuinely cared about her and wanted to help her find the justice she craved.

Instinct told her that he had his own reasons to hunt down the man who'd inhabited the same world as their fathers.

Yes, their fathers might have worked on different sides of the law—Stella's police sergeant dad catching the criminals while Hagen's defense attorney dad tried to release them—but they had mingled in the same circles and known the same people.

And yet, each time the conversation had approached Hagen's father last night, he'd pulled away, shut it down. As long as he didn't want to discuss it, Stella struggled to trust him. She'd been so open with her feelings...

"It's just...it bothers me, you know? Seeing him with a family. When I thought he was dead, it hurt, but I wasn't angry with him. Getting murdered wasn't his choice. But while I was mourning, he was watching his kids grow up, taking vacations with his wife, playing with his grandchildren. Now I just feel..."

"Abandoned?"

Did Hagen even know how close to the center he'd hit that target? If he did, she hadn't been able to tell by either his words or actions...

Hagen patted her arm. The contact was friendly and warm, but in its brevity, distant and formal. "I get it. He was your dad's partner. It was natural you'd want someone like him around after your dad was killed."

"Is that what happened to you? Did you have—"

"Listen." His bottle clanked on the counter. "The answers are in Atlanta, so that's where we need to be. We've got a few days of paperwork ahead of us, but assuming Tennessee's population of psychopaths and disgruntled ex-cheerleaders take a break through the weekend, once we're done, we can head back down there. This time we won't waste a second. We on?"

She hadn't been able to think of a good reason to say no.

Did she really want to tell him no?

She took a long sip of her hot chocolate and returned the cup to the holder. Tapping her thumb on the steering wheel, her gaze remained on the rearview mirror a little longer than usual.

She'd been followed recently. An SUV trailed them to Atlanta. Then, at some point, it turned into an old, beat-up Camry. But she hadn't seen the Toyota when she'd returned home last night. And there was no sign of the car now as she headed to the office.

Maybe the tail had given up. Part of her hoped she'd still catch sight of whoever it was and could force some answers. Part of her was relieved.

Relief eased some of the morning tension, letting her thoughts drift back to Hagen.

When they had taken down their suspect yesterday, she'd trusted her fellow agent utterly. She'd pulled out her gun and moved to where the killer was waiting. She hadn't even bothered to look back to make sure Hagen had followed. She *knew* he would be there. He had her back.

She took another long sip of hot chocolate. Some of the chocolate had collected at the bottom of the cup, giving the drink a bitter aftertaste.

The traffic cleared. She slipped the cup back into its holder and put her foot down.

But at times, instead of being the support she needed, Hagen was a weight she was forced to bear. A weight she was constantly shifting on her back to maintain balance lest she drop it.

"And he shouldn't be." She spoke aloud as she pulled into the parking garage of the FBI's Resident Agency. "I need to know he's there with me. *For* me. And, if not for me alone, *why* he's there."

She turned off the engine and reached for the cup again. It was empty.

"Nuts."

Stella took her bag with its pair of giant cookies and climbed out of the SUV. She hated feeling this way, unsure of her direction.

Her brain told her one thing. Hagen was exactly the help she needed, a trained FBI agent who cared about her. A friend who brought some benefits.

But her heart shouted something else, that he was secretive and dark, hiding something she needed to know.

She locked the doors to her 4Runner and swung her bag over her shoulder.

Stella exhaled deeply and checked her watch. She was early. The rest of the team wouldn't be in for another twenty minutes or so, but Stella had wanted to get a start on the day.

So much paperwork had built up over the last few weeks.

She'd write up her interviews, complete all the forms waiting on her, focus on what she needed to do, and check out at the end of the day all caught up. The monotony wasn't appealing, but it was a nice change from confronting killers.

Plus, human resources was interviewing and assessing new applicants, so it was going to be all bureaucracy round the clock at the Agency today.

And it looked like one of those applicants, a woman wearing a knee-length skirt and peachy pumps, was headed inside. The woman had a slight limp. A twinge of sympathy struck Stella in the chest.

New shoes, huh? Maybe that's what's up with the limp?

A tall man in baggy jeans and a tight, white t-shirt that stretched across the muscles of his broad chest headed out of the garage toward the building site at the end of the road. He was carrying a backpack over a shoulder as he rushed past Stella.

She assessed him until he disappeared. She'd always been a people watcher by nature, which served her well as her livelihood *and her life* depended on her ability to discern evil from good.

Was Tight White simply late for work? Was he sneaking home after a late-night bender? Rushing to the store to pick up milk for his family? Odds were, he was doing something innocent like the majority of Nashvillians. Probably. She hoped.

Digging in her bag for her entry badge, Stella halted her musing so she could open the door to the Nashville Resident Agency. She was getting ready to swipe when a yellow piece of paper secured to the door by a piece of duct tape caught her attention. It wasn't the first memo of its kind, and it resembled the kind a maintenance person would put up to provide a warning.

Maybe someone had broken the lock. Maybe the office was closed for the day, and she'd have to go home and have the entire day off instead of doing paperwork.

Ha. Fat chance.

She drew closer. The writing on the memo wasn't typed out like normal, though. This one boasted capital letters, each word scrawled but clear.

What Are You Afraid Of, Paul Slade?

What the hell?

Stella glanced around the parking garage. She still had a good view of the street level beyond the red and white arms of the entry barriers. Vehicles clipped by at a steady pace. A few pedestrians crossed the road at the intersection across the way. Nothing appeared out of the ordinary. No one paused to watch her reaction.

She peered through the windshields of the handful of parked cars. They were all empty.

Feeling a little overly cautious, she leaned down to check if anyone, or anything, was hiding under a vehicle.

Nothing.

Stella read the memo again.

She'd never seen her boss, Supervisory Special Agent Paul Slade, afraid of anything. He'd been a little overly sensitive during their recent case involving teenage girls. Not that she could blame him—he had three daughters. But she wouldn't call him *afraid*.

The question struck her as odd. Stella considered it for a second.

What was *she* afraid of?

Did she fear the people who had killed her father since she knew they might kill her, too, if she got too close to the truth?

No.

Stella wasn't afraid of them, whoever they were. Her biggest concern about those killers wasn't what they might do, but the possible emptiness that could follow finding them. She feared that hole could be dark and unending.

She wasn't afraid of killers or psychos or monster clowns from outer space.

The thought of losing someone else she loved was terrifying.

She'd lost her father to a drug gang and dirty cops. She'd lost her brother to cancer. Apart from her mother, she'd lost everyone she'd ever loved.

Her mother.

The thought of losing her mom seemed to open a great hole just in front of her feet, a dark space that could suck her down and steal all remaining hope. She shook her head. Her mom was fine. Her stepdad wasn't in great shape, but he was okay after the heart attack too. At least that's what her mom had said.

Enough.

The question was so strange, and the handwriting was almost threatening. She felt the need to treat it as potential evidence. Stella pulled out her phone and snapped a picture. Then she went back to her 4Runner and yanked out a small forensics kit she kept in the back seat.

Back at the door, she used a pair of tweezers to carefully remove the tape from the door, keeping everything intact. Then she dropped the yellow paper into a clear evidence bag and sealed it.

Why the hell is someone asking what Slade is afraid of?

She pushed the door open and carried the memo inside. It was probably a joke. A bad joke.

But maybe not.

3

Special Agent Hagen Yates pulled his cherry red Corvette into the parking space next to Stella's dark gray Toyota 4Runner. Her choice of vehicle always made him smile. It fit her perfectly. Powerful. Unstoppable. And easy to look at. Reliable too.

He shut off the engine but remained in his seat, one arm resting against the door while he cursed himself for the hundredth time that morning.

I'm an idiot. I should have opened up to her.

Stella wasn't stupid. She had to know he'd been holding back about his own past, and that knowledge would lead her to hold more of herself back too.

He'd come so close to telling her everything, but habit and fear of being hurt kept his mouth closed. Well, not completely. To his surprise, he talked about his past more than he'd ever done with anyone else. He'd told her about his father's meetings with local criminals and the respect they held for the magician who could wave a legal brief like a wand and make their biggest crimes disappear.

Their fathers had worked similar cases in Memphis and had run in the same circles. Stella's dad along the periphery. Hagen's dad sometimes right smack in the middle.

Were the two deaths related? His gut insisted they were.

Both men navigated the same criminals. Both died from a bullet. Both tied to drug investigations. He didn't have anything concrete yet, so he kept his thoughts to himself.

But whenever Stella steered the conversation toward his father's murder, Hagen shifted direction. Changed the subject. Pulled away.

Yep...a damn idiot.

Withdrawal was a habit. It was a good one. He was sure it was. The rage that burned deep inside him, that fire demanding justice, was too bright and too hot for anyone else to see...feel...touch.

Stella's goal in finding her father's killer was to arrest him. Bring him to legal justice. Give him his day in court. Her intent was noble and moral.

And wrong.

With the right lawyer, the biggest crooks found loopholes that kept them out of trouble and away from prison.

If Stella did things her way, her father's killer—possibly *their* fathers' killer—would get nothing worse than a short stay in a comfortable prison. Free bed and board with the ability to run his empire from a cell. That wasn't justice. It certainly wasn't enough.

Vindicta.

The tattoo ran between his shoulder blades. Its call for vengeance still burned as much as it did the day the tattooist carved it into his skin.

Hagen had his own plan, and he needed to stick to it.

Climbing out of the Corvette, he slammed the door and strode into the resident office after swiping his key card.

Stella was already at her desk. His stomach tightened a little. She looked good, even first thing on a Friday morning. Her long, brown hair was pulled back into her signature ponytail. It shimmered as it caught the morning light shining through the office window just right. Her short-sleeved blouse showed off her slim figure, and when her eyes caught his, he could see the golden flecks scattered through her brown irises.

His stomach tightened even more. He ignored it. "Morning."

She gave him a short nod. "Hey."

He should say something else, crack a joke about last night's food. His mouth opened, but nothing came out.

What a fool.

He passed behind her and headed to his own desk in the corner. She turned back to her monitor, rubbing the back of her neck.

Hagen breathed out slowly. He hadn't been tongue-tied like this since he was fourteen years old and had asked the tall, blond freshman track star on a date. She'd agreed, and he'd never struggled for words since. He forced himself to look away.

Go talk to her.

He didn't need to talk about his dad, but he needed to keep Stella close. If he had a prayer's chance of finding the people responsible for his father's murder, she was his best bet.

He mentally girded his loins and stood. "Hey, Stella. I'm grabbing a coffee from the machine. You want a hot chocolate?"

She twisted in her chair. "No. I'm good, thanks. Just had one."

"With marshmallows?"

She grinned. "Just foam. Lots of foam."

He crossed to the machine and swiped his card. The cup dropped. As he waited for the machine to finish gurgling and spit the thick, black espresso into the cup, he leaned against the wall.

"You know, without the marshmallows, it's not—"

The office door swung open, and Special Agent Chloe Drake strode in. Her arm was still in a sling, recovering from a gunshot wound to her shoulder. She'd been grouchy for about three weeks now.

Hagen had an urge to give Chloe a friendly pat on her good arm, but she'd probably give him a roundhouse kick in return.

Paul Slade followed, closing the door behind him. The resident office's supervisory special agent was tall, with ice-blue eyes and graying brown hair cropped close to the scalp. The cut did little to hide his deepening middle age.

Hagen gave them both a quiet, "Morning."

Before either had a chance to respond, Stella was out of her seat and walking toward Slade with an evidence bag in her hands. "Sir."

Hagen frowned as he took his coffee from the machine. The last case was closed. There was nothing he knew of that Stella needed to run past Slade.

Unless she was going to ask for some time off to follow her own investigation.

If she planned to do that, he needed to move fast to join her.

Slade stopped in the short hallway leading to his office. He jammed his hands into the pockets of his suit and nodded at the yellow sheet in Stella's hand. "What have you got there?"

Hagen sipped his coffee. It was over brewed and bitter, the result of too many cheap Robusta beans badly ground and exposed to the air for too long. He frowned but sipped again.

Stella lifted the clear bag with her fingertips. It flapped slightly in the breeze from the air conditioner. "Found this on the door this morning."

Slade pulled his reading glasses from his jacket pocket and pushed them onto his nose. They made him look about ten years older, which just about put Slade into retirement age. No wonder he preferred to keep them in his pocket rather than near his face.

He took the bag from Stella's hand and read the yellow sheet of paper inside. "'What are you afraid of, Paul Slade?'"

Hagen lowered his cup.

What the hell is that?

Chloe had been halfway to her desk. She stopped and turned back. Slade flipped the bag over, peered at the reverse side, then flipped it around again. He pushed his glasses down his nose.

"Where did you say you found this?"

Stella waved in the general direction of the parking garage. "It was stuck on the garage entrance door this morning."

"And you didn't see who put it there?"

Stella shook her head.

The door opened again. Mac came in. She glanced at Slade and her cheeks reddened, highlighting her white-blond hair. "Sorry I'm a bit late. The traffic was..." She paused, taking in the crowd of agents around the yellow paper. "Whoa. What's that all about? Bomb threat?"

Slade lifted the evidence bag. "Someone wants to know what I'm afraid of."

Hagen tossed his empty cup into the recycling bin. "The dark. Everyone knows that."

Slade peered at him over the top of his glasses. "Speak for

yourself, Hagen. I thrive in the dark. No, what frightens me is you all not getting your FD-302s in on time."

Hagen grimaced. He had a giant pile of interview notes he needed to summarize and stuff into those forms. The thought didn't warm his heart. Even though it was probably nothing, the paper dangling from Slade's fingertips offered a potential boredom breaker. "That note could be a threat. We should look into it."

Slade handed Mac the evidence bag. "It's probably nothing, but let's give it to security. Since you said the 'bomb' word, you win the opportunity to deliver it."

Mac rolled her eyes but took the bag.

Chloe jabbed a finger toward Mac's office. "We should take a look at the security cameras anyway. See if we can spot anything."

Slade packed his glasses back into his pocket. "You get five minutes, but then straight back to your desks. Not even a note from your mom is going to get you out of paperwork today."

Chloe flashed a smile and followed Mac into her office.

"I think another set of eyes would be useful." Hagen followed Chloe. Taking his lead, Stella was right behind him. The four of them crowded around Mac's desk. She set the threat to the side before bringing up the security footage surrounding the building.

To Hagen's surprise, Slade drifted in as well.

The SSA pointed to the box in the top left corner. "Just focus on that one, the one that shows the door."

Mac made the box bigger and rewound the footage. On the screen, Mac, then Slade, Chloe, and Hagen all walked backward out of the office. Stella followed. She appeared to stick the note to the door before striding in reverse away from the building.

Hagen nudged her. "Why'd you do it, Stella? You could've just asked him."

Stella rolled her eyes.

Mac's laugh stopped short. "There."

She hit play. A broad-chested figure with a cap worn low on his head approached. He had on jeans and a dark blue work jacket of some kind. When he reached the door, he swung a backpack from his shoulder, pulled out the note, and a roll of duct tape.

Moving quickly, he cut the tape with a large knife, stuck it to the door, and strode away.

"He knows he can just rip duct tape, right?" Stella leaned closer to the feed, as if she could see the man's face if she stared hard enough.

Beside her, Hagen also leaned in. "I think he's wearing gloves. Harder to rip tape when it's catching on material."

Stella tapped the screen. "Can you go back and zoom in?"

Mac rewound the feed. "Tell me when."

The guy walked back in frame, reversing his steps until he was once again facing the door. Stella held up a hand. "Stop."

Mac zoomed in until only the man's head and torso were on the screen. "That's good."

The room was silent as Stella studied the image. When thirty seconds had passed, Hagen started to get annoyed. "What—?"

Stella held up a hand. "I saw him." Her voice lacked conviction, though. "Except he wasn't wearing a jacket or a hat. The backpack's the same, though."

Hagen frowned. "What did he look like?"

"He was looking the other way, so I didn't see his face. Seemed to be in a hurry."

Slade's glasses practically fell off the tip of his sharp nose. He shoved them up. "Is he on any other cameras?"

Mac shrugged. "That's all we got. Just a minute. Let's try this."

She cycled through the local traffic cameras and the remaining security footage but found nothing but people crossing the road and waiting for the lights to change. She brought up a map of connections to local cell towers and watched the dots move across the screen.

"I can't see anything unusual here."

Stella squinted at the monitor. "Isn't that unusual in itself? Someone just stuck a threat to the door of an FBI office, and their movements don't stand out on security footage or cell phone data?"

Chloe nodded, agreeing with Stella.

"He's a cunning dude. That's professional-level thinking, that is." Hagen studied Stella. There she was, thinking smart again. He really did need to keep her close. He couldn't let her get to Joel without him. She'd never give him a second chance. Or maybe Stella really, really didn't want to spend all day at the computer.

"Or could be he's just some idiot fooling around." Slade tapped a knuckle against the desk as Mac reached for her phone. "Now, why don't you all—"

"It's a bit specific for some idiot fooling around." Stella pulled away from the monitor and stretched her back. "They put your name on it."

"Yeah, I got a funny feeling about this." Chloe indicated the note with a brief nod. "This looks like a threat to me."

Slade stepped back from the desk and stood straight. "And I've got a funny feeling you're all looking for a way to avoid your paperwork. There's no crime here. I'm not worried about some idiot taping a name they probably found on Google to the parking garage door of the FBI, and neither should you be. We've all got enough to do without investigating jumbo-sized sticky notes. Now, go on back to work. All of you."

Chloe huffed and picked up her bag before heading to her desk. Slade and Hagen followed her out.

Hagen could almost hear his interview forms calling to him from his computer.

Stella stopped when she reached the doorway. "Mac, I've got something for you. Just a sec."

Hagen was just able to hear Mac's quiet reply. "And I've got something for you too. You'll want to hear this."

4

When Stella realized Hagen was dawdling on his way back to his desk, she shook her head. Everyone was procrastinating this morning. Well, everyone but Special Agents Martin Lin and Caleb Hudson, who'd been called out on another case.

"Those interview summaries won't write themselves, you know."

Hagen lifted an eyebrow. "I thought you were an optimist. I'm hoping if I walk slowly enough to my desk, by the time I get there, little elves will have written and submitted them for me."

"Yeah, I don't think that's gonna work." Stella rummaged in her bag until she found the two giant cookies she'd bought earlier. "But if it does happen, ask them to write mine for me."

With a bright smile, she closed the door to Mac's office right in his face. The cyber tech looked up from her monitor, her gaze falling on the cookies.

"Whoa, where did you get those? They look big enough to pique Area 51's interest."

Stella slid one across the desk and dropped into the chair opposite Mac. "From the café beneath my apartment. I think they special order them for me. By the truckload." She popped a chunk of cookie into her mouth, closing her eyes at the burst of flavor.

Mac took a bite. "Mmm. Tell them to order two truckloads next time." Mouth full, her expression turned serious, and she lowered her voice. "You still being followed?"

Stella swallowed. The chocolate no longer tasted as sweet as it had a moment before. Discovering she'd been shadowed during the last case had both creeped her out and intrigued her. Things were *afoot*, as a certain great detective would say. "I don't think so. No, I didn't see anyone this morning. That's a good thing, right?"

Mac broke off another piece of cookie. She thought before she answered. "I…doubt it. Could mean they've gotten better. More professional."

"Or they've gotten bored and moved on to someone else." Stella hoped her calm demeanor would be contagious.

Mac squashed a crumb between her fingers. Her fidgety behavior told Stella more than words ever could. "I don't think so." Her voice was slow and quiet, as though something heavy had seeped into her brain.

"What's going on? What do you have to tell me?"

Mac hesitated. She folded over the edge of the cookie bag and set it on one side of the desk. "When you told me Joel Ramirez was alive, I dug around a bit into the circumstances of his death. He was shot answering a 911 call, and his body was cremated."

Stella knew this. Joel's was the third funeral she'd attended in three years, the third death of someone close to her before she was sixteen years old. She remembered the seats at the funeral, the rows of uniforms with stripes and stars and gloves filling every single one, or so it seemed. The same kinds of speeches she had heard just a year earlier at her father's funeral were recycled at Joel's. The same notes of "Amazing Grace" filled the hall.

And she recalled the numbness that had seeped into her bones. It made the room seem hazy and distant. Her only emotion was a dim knowledge that she would be here again. And soon again after that. And again, until everyone she ever loved was dead and gone.

Because that was what happened to the people she loved.

She grew attached to them. She depended on them.

And they died.

Stella chewed her cookie. "I know. I was there."

Mac pushed harder on the crumb. "Yeah. And we now know Joel wasn't."

Stella winced. In the shock of encountering a living Uncle Joel, she hadn't realized how absurd the funeral must have been. All those people, the great and good of the Memphis Police Department, gathered to say a final farewell to a guy enjoying a beer with his secret family just a state away.

"It's insane."

Mac shook her head. "No. But it's a lot of work and a lot of deception. What's the payoff? Why did someone want the world to believe Joel Ramirez was dead?"

Stella's gaze met Mac's. A light seemed to come on in her head like electricity ramping up through a faulty wire that was only now coming back to life. Sometimes, Mac knew exactly which questions to ask.

"Do you know why?"

Mac flicked the cookie crumb off the desk. "I checked the crematorium's records. There was no cremation of any middle-aged man that day. And only one organization would have gone to the trouble of faking a death as carefully as this."

The light in Stella's head burned brightly. "Witness Protection."

Mac nodded. "Right. So I called my contact. They confirmed that Joel went into the program."

Stella lifted her eyebrows. That was not the kind of information you could pick up with a quick search in the FBI archives.

"How did you—?"

Mac raised a hand. "I…it doesn't matter. Let's just say I owe them one. Anyway, that was all I could get. My contact wouldn't tell me why Joel Ramirez went into witness protection. I'm guessing they don't know. That's something you'll have to dig up. Or we will."

"Right." Stella broke off another piece of cookie, studying the chips as a hundred questions swirled through her mind.

So Joel was in witness protection. He must've seen something. He must know something. And maybe—probably—that something must connect to her father's death.

It has to.

Mac retrieved her cookie and broke off another piece. "You realize this gives you a big problem."

Stella snorted out a laugh. "Just one?"

"Well, two then. Two big ones."

"Hm." Stella took a deep breath. "How do I discover what Joel knows without the U.S. Marshals finding out?"

"Right. And without whoever Joel is hiding from discovering what you're doing."

5
―――

Shhnk.
The sound of a spade as the edge sliced into the ground was so satisfying. Like you'd taken on the earth and won. Cut it into pieces. You'd carved a great chunk out of its flesh and could keep on cutting until you pulled out its heart.

Yeah, it was good work, digging. Like chopping wood and hammering nails. Work like that was food for the soul. Made you feel alive.

Earth filled the spade, and I heaved it over the side of the hole.

Thump.

Some of the dirt flew back in the breeze. Bits landed in the sweat on my neck and dusted my shoulders.

Sweat, a little dirt. It's all good for you. Makes a man proud.

I wasn't one of those fellers with soft, clean hands and arms like sticks. The kind of man other men didn't take seriously.

I was someone to take seriously.

Dirt smeared across my forehead as I wiped my brow. Everything was sticky. Probably should've dug in the shade.

The barn was right there, not ten yards away. But the shadow thrown by the midday sun was little more than a thin strip next to the wall.

Too close, man. Too close.

Shhnk.

That deputy. He wasn't a man you could take seriously. A traffic cop. Such a bullshit job. Spending his nights stopping people for going a little faster than they should. Taking their money for a small breach of a rule no man in his right mind would pay attention to anyway.

Just another form of highway robbery. That's what it was.

Still...

Thump.

He was law enforcement. He should've had some spirit, a backbone. Some *cojones*. Man, he'd been useless.

I leaned on my spade and wiped the sweat from my brow again. The sun was just too much. Like an oven, it was. Like Iraq...

A big, orange ball burst under my feet and sent me flying backward, upside down, toppling, rolling.

I gasped and shook my head.

The heat, man. The heat.

Wouldn't want to be doing this work for too much longer.

Shhnk.

That deputy, he hadn't had any courage at all. I poured those spiders over him, and he just screamed and screamed. Like a child. That's what he sounded like. A little girl. Half-expected him to cry for his mommy.

Thump.

I breathed out hard. Sweat ran down the back of my neck. I peeled off my t-shirt and hurled it onto the ground. The air was fresh on my skin. Made me shiver a little with its kiss.

Man, this work wasn't easy. I'd been out here for a couple

of hours already, and the hole barely reached past my knees. Dude was gonna have to make do with less than six feet of grave. Time was a-ticking. Gotta stay on schedule, to the minute. Punctuality mattered.

Shhnk.

Not like he deserved the whole six feet. That was what a *man* deserved. A six-foot hole and a proper stone on top.

Thump.

I leaned on the spade again and looked toward the bulge under the tarp next to the hole.

"That's not what you're getting, feller. You ain't even gettin' three feet. But don't worry. There'll be enough spiders in there for you."

I laughed.

Shhnk.

"Spiders. You were supposed to be a sheriff's deputy."

Thump.

"Brave. Fearless. Upstanding. Spiders! At your age. Jeez, even children get over that."

Shhnk. Thump.

That'd have to do. It would do for this dude.

I stepped out of the hole and jammed the spade into the ground.

Though I gotta admit, them spiders weren't the prettiest critters in the world. Took me a while to build up a collection like that. Had to drive around, digging through abandoned barns and woodpiles. Still had a few left over in a corner of the barn.

Dealing with them afterward had been a mess. Caught what I could for future use, if needed. Spade got most of the faster ones. Had to stomp a few. And dealing with them afterward. Man, what a mess.

Some of those old boys probably took up under my porch and would surely give a delivery guy a surprise. He probably wouldn't have an allergy like the deputy did, though. Guess that was what had made him so scared. Ended my fun before it really got started.

The thought sent a little shiver through me. I felt sorry for him, almost. But a law enforcement officer was supposed to overcome his fears. That's what courage meant—face your fear and do what's necessary.

Still, I could've done with finishing the job earlier, what with having another mission to complete first thing in the morning. But that's how it was, sometimes. You learned to operate on minimal sleep. Grab a cold shower, a couple of slaps on the cheeks, and an energy drink, and away you went.

Eight hours in the sack? Sleep was for the weak.

I yawned and scratched the back of my neck. The deputy's body sprawled at my feet, wrapped in the tarp. I grabbed the corner and pulled.

"Hnn."

Dude was heavier than I'd imagined. Had taken a ton of energy to drag him out of the barn once I'd tipped him out of the box. That was probably why I'd found digging his hole so hard.

Not much farther to go now.

I bent my back and tugged harder. He slid across the ground.

My heel landed on the edge of the hole. I slipped and stumbled into the shallow grave. "Dammit."

Didn't matter none. Maybe it would even make the job easier. I grabbed the tarp again and pulled.

Ker-thump.

The body landed at my feet. That did it.

What a waste. Such a shame. That was a good tarp. Could've used that for all sorts of things. Shame to bury it just to keep a dead deputy covered.

I took the edge again and rolled the deputy out of the plastic.

He didn't look so good. His face was a strange shade of blue. His lips were like half-inflated balloons, and his tongue stuck out of the front of his mouth like a half-sucked popsicle. The bites on his cheeks and his hands had swollen into sharp little cones like tiny, angry volcanoes.

I put my hands on my hips and spoke quietly. "Look at you. Lying there now. That was all you had to do, just lie there in that box, and let the spiders walk all over. If you could've managed that, I might just have let you go. You'd have shown yourself worthy."

I reached for the spade and loaded it up with earth.

"But you couldn't do that, could you? Couldn't face your fears."

I swung the spade. *Thump.*

"And they told me I couldn't be a deputy. That I didn't have what it takes."

Shhnk.

"They're the ones who don't have what it takes. They don't even have what it takes to find one of their own."

Thump.

I leaned on the spade and smiled. "Let's see if the next one does any better."

6

Stella sat at her desk and flipped a page in her notebook. There, in front of her, were the words of Susie Mostrom, the gossipy mother of a murdered teenage girl named Olivia. The cheerleader's future had seemed bright. She was a talented athlete who had been accepted to Florida State. She was the captain of her cheerleading squad.

But in Stella's notebook, all the pain and shock the girl had encountered were reduced to a few lines of blue ink on a white sheet.

She'd convert those words into black letters on a screen, which would then be stored away on a hard drive somewhere. That conversation, the words that led Stella and Hagen to her daughter's killer, would probably never be seen again. But Susie Mostrom's pain would go on, visible to everyone who met her.

Her fingers clacked across the keyboard.

At the desk opposite, Chloe peeked up from her own computer. "Typing like a demon there, Stella. You'd have made an excellent secretary."

Stella frowned. Chloe could be sharp sometimes, but Stella knew she could trust the prickly agent.

She'd been there when Chloe had taken a bullet, and she'd seen Chloe bounce right back to work. Stella wasn't sure whether the shot had left any deeper scars, but she couldn't help but admire her colleague's resilience.

And her constant attempts to get under Stella's skin.

Stella resumed typing. "Wouldn't work. The boss would tell me to make coffee. I'd put in cocoa powder instead of those smelly beans, everyone would fall asleep at their desks, and nothing would get done. It'd be a disaster. That's why I had to give up my dream of secretarial school and settle for a life at the FBI."

Chloe almost smiled. "Fair enough. We all have to make sacrifices. Rate you're typing, though, you'll be done by lunchtime."

"I don't know about that. I can't read my own writing." Stella flicked through the pages of her notebook, looking for context clues for one word she couldn't decipher. She'd filled one sheet after another with her scrawled handwriting. She'd never picked up the ability to write both fast and legibly. "Plus, I've got enough notes here to keep me busy for a week."

"Lucky you."

The sarcasm was clear. Stella glanced over at Chloe. The injured agent pecked at her keyboard with one finger on her uninjured side.

Chloe saw Stella looking at her and stopped typing. "What I mean is, at least you've got something to type up. I spent most of last week sitting outside a high school, drinking coffee, and trying to reassure frightened parents. It was you and Hagen who did most of the work. Again."

"Now, come on. That's not—"

"'Course it is." Chloe pulled her chair closer. "I'm not

complaining. Slade made the right call." She lifted her left arm as far as the sling would allow and winced. "I'm still not firing on all cylinders, and you got the job done. You two make a good pair."

Special Agent Ander Bennett looked up from his desk at the end of the room. He appeared very interested in her response.

Mortified, Stella held up a hand. "We're not—"

Chloe leaned closer and lowered her voice. "I hear you two spent a night in Atlanta together. Nice. But listen, I gotta tell you. Just because the FBI doesn't have any clear rules about workplace relationships doesn't mean an office fling can't become a problem." She slid her eyes over to Hagen's desk. "Especially with him."

Pissed, Stella glanced around. *People in the office are talking already.*

"That's not what—"

Something flew from the back of the room. It arced over the desks, sailed over the computers, and clattered into the side of Chloe's head. She spun in her chair as the paper ball rolled under the desk.

"Hey!"

Grinning, Ander waved his phone. "Listen to this. Just got a text from a friend at the fire department in Pelham."

Chloe rubbed her temple. "You got a friend, Ander? That's nice. Do you throw your garbage at him too?" She picked up the ball and lobbed it back his way.

He batted it away with his phone. "And it's past the fences!" Chloe crumpled up a sheet from her legal pad.

Ander held up a hand to stop her. "But listen up. He found a yellow note on the door of his station this morning. It said, 'What are you afraid of, Mick Ackhurst?'"

Stella's stomach tightened.

One might be a joke.

Killer Memo   41

Two meant a plan was in the works.

Chloe leaned forward, clearly thinking the same thing as Stella. "He send you a picture?"

"Yeah." Ander tapped his phone. "Sharing it with you now."

A double ping told Stella both she and Chloe had received the file. The memo appeared identical to the one she'd found on the door of the resident office. The same yellow sheet of paper and the same wide, silver duct tape around the edges.

Chloe scowled at her phone. "That is certainly weird. Your buddy send it to the sheriff's office?" She glanced over at Stella. "Because we could follow up, you know? Head out there. Away from the office."

Stella looked from her almost illegible notebook to her screen and back to Chloe. "Yes. It seems like something to check into."

Ander shook his head. His long, blond curls bounced around his ears. "No way, you two. If anyone's getting away from these forms, it's gonna be me. My friend, my lead."

"Hey, Knox." Slade stood in the office doorway, one hand wrapped around the jamb. "Got a job for you."

Chloe swiveled her chair around and eyed their supervisor. "Hope for your sake it's not making coffee."

"What?" Slade frowned, then shook his head, visibly deciding not to engage. "No. Just heard from the sheriff's office in Pelham. Sheriff Marlowe's wife is a friend of my wife. Poor guy's short-staffed. A deputy didn't come home after his night shift. He's probably loading up on pancakes somewhere or sleeping off a late binge. Still, something's bugging me about it. See if there's any more news. Just touch base."

"Sir, Ander has something I think we should follow up on—"

Another sheet of crumpled paper hit Chloe mid-sentence. But Slade was already gone.

Stella pulled up the number and dialed. "Pelham Sheriff's Office. Deputy Rice speaking."

"This is Special Agent Stella Knox of the FBI's Nashville Resident Agency. I understand you've got a deputy missing?"

The person on the end of the line cleared her throat. "Yeah, just a minute. I'll put you through to Sheriff Marlowe."

The phone rang and rang again. Stella sighed as the elevator music clicked on. She flipped to a new blank page in her notebook. As the music droned on, a tickle of irritation built up in her guts.

Hey, I'm trying to help you guys out here. I've got a ton of witness—

"Sheriff Marlowe." The voice was deep, confident.

"Sheriff, this is Special Agent Stella Knox of the FBI—"

"You're calling about Carlos?"

Stella picked up her pen. "Is Carlos your missing deputy?"

"Yeah. Carlos Guerrero. Was on traffic duty last night and last report from him was around two a.m. His wife called a couple hours ago. He didn't come home."

Stella's hand drifted toward her gold ear stud. Her father had given her the earrings for her fourteenth birthday. She twisted it as she thought. "Is he the type to always head straight home after a shift?"

"Yeah, that guy's straight as an arrow. I'm guessing he's just sleeping it off at the back of a bar somewhere, but, man, that'd be strange behavior for him. I hope it's nothing worse than that."

"Me too."

Sheriff Marlowe chuckled, but the sound didn't last long. "Y'know, it's funny. Someone asked me today what I'm afraid of. The answer to that question is what it's always been. I'm scared of losing an officer under my command."

Stella's hand dropped from her ear, and she sat straight up. "Someone asked you what you're afraid of? Who asked you that?"

At Stella's question, Chloe's finger froze over her keyboard.

Ander pushed out of his chair and stood.

Sheriff Marlowe's deep voice sounded in Stella's ear. "That's the funny thing. I don't know. It was on a note on the door this morning."

7

Fire Inspector Veronica Trang slid the form across the desk and tapped the sheet three times with her finger. "The fire inspection is done. Looks like you've got some work to do."

Greg Collins, owner of Rugz Textiles, glared at the red Xs on the form. The factory owner's face reddened, making the graying blond beard barely covering his jowls look even lighter. His fat fingers curled into the palms of his hands.

Veronica stood there, unmoving. Today, she appeared to be a mild-mannered fire safety inspector. But for more than ten years, she had fought fires. She'd run into burning buildings, confronted hysterical victims at roadside accidents, and seen rooms explode seconds after she'd left them. At five-five, she might not have been as tall as other firefighters, or have all their upper body strength, but she could beat every one of them any day when it came to courage.

She didn't even blink.

Collins took a deep breath. "Just who the hell do you think you are, woman?" Spittle flew from his lips.

His voice would have intimidated most people. To Veronica, he just sounded like every man who had ever told her a woman couldn't be a fire inspector, couldn't be a firefighter, wouldn't get into college, couldn't do this, and shouldn't do that.

She spoke calmly. "I'm the fire inspector. And you're the guy who's going to fix all those problems and do it all within the next thirty days. Otherwise, I become the woman who is shutting you down."

Collins pushed to his feet, his fists resting on the desk, whitening his knuckles. "Like hell I am."

Veronica sighed. She'd heard this before, but thankfully not too often. "So don't. Instead, you'll be the guy who gets three Class C misdemeanors and ninety days in a cell with four guys twice your size."

The chances of imprisonment for fire violations were pretty small, but the threat was usually enough to make even the most recalcitrant of business owners back down. Most just wanted to cut corners and protect their profits. Few were really looking for a fight.

But Greg Collins didn't back down. He glared at her with enough heat to start a forest fire.

"You don't know who the hell you're dealing with, missy!" His shout made the windows in his office rattle.

Veronica glanced over her shoulder through the picture window showing a panoramic view of the textile factory. Behind her, rows and rows of sewing machines whirred and clicked and buzzed as women—and it was all women, all immigrants—pushed cloth under needles in return for "pay by the piece."

No one who knew their rights would agree to work in a place like this. Those women were definitely getting less than minimum wage while working in a shop with no windows and little ventilation.

And all for a man like Greg Collins.

At the end of one of the rows, two women laughed, though Veronica couldn't hear them in the sound-proofed office. Collins saw the women too. He stormed around his desk, yanked the door open, and yelled loud enough to drown out the sound of the work, which was impressive because the place was growling with machinery.

The language he used. The only word in Spanish he threw in was *"puta,"* and he stuffed it between every other English swearword in the dictionary.

The two women stopped laughing and got straight back to work. But what really stood out—what made Veronica want to pick up her form, restart her inspection, and find a half dozen more reasons to give Collins a hard time—was that no one else reacted. None of the other women so much as took their eyes off their sewing machines, which buzzed and clicked and whirred. They'd seen this behavior before and learned to ignore it.

Veronica swore under her breath. Employment law wasn't her job. Someone else would need to get in here. Her job was to enforce the fire code.

And she was going to make damn sure she did.

Collins slammed the door shut and stormed back to his chair. He lifted one large hand and extended his finger. "I served my country. Three tours in Iraq. That's what I did. And now I find that you...you...you government goons and your dumbass regulations are trying to put hardworking Americans like me out of business."

Pressure grew in Veronica's chest like boiling oil on the edge of an explosion. She picked up the form off the desk and gestured for him to follow her. "Come with me."

He followed, as she knew he would. She led him to the fuse box and showed him the bare wires, the burnt-out fuses, and the charring on the circuit breakers.

Oily rags lay next to an electricity outlet against the wall, just waiting for a spark.

Finally, she stomped past the sewing machines to the fire door at the end of the room. The door was barely visible behind piles of boxes blocking the way.

She wasn't finished. Pointing at the ceiling, she saved the best for last. "When you bought this building, you were informed that the sprinkler system didn't meet the new codes, especially with the number of employees you have working inside this building."

"I—"

Veronica faced him, her jaw set. "If there's a fire in this place, and there *will* be a fire in this place, everyone here will die. You've got...how many? Sixty women here. That's sixty dead people. Sixty counts of manslaughter because you were too damn cheap to fix a fuse box and sprinkler system and keep this place clean."

"You can't—"

She slammed the form against his chest. "Fix it."

Instead of giving him the punch in the face he deserved, she stormed out.

The heat in her chest still boiled. Her footsteps echoed off the corridor's concrete walls.

That guy. The nerve of him.

Halfway down the corridor, a fluorescent tube flickered, briefly illuminating an arc of dusty wires hanging from the ceiling.

Veronica cursed. This place was a death trap. Records showed it had once been used to make and store chemicals. The thick walls and maze of corridors were built to withstand leaks and explosions from compounds reacting from a bad mix.

Thank God it's not used for that anymore.

Now it was a harmless textile factory.

Yeah, tell that to the Greenwich Village industrial fire women.

A sweatshop. That's what this place was. A modern sweatshop.

Veronica reached a junction and hesitated. Had she gone left or right when she'd come in from the parking lot? She couldn't remember.

Left. She was sure she'd gone left.

Footsteps sounded somewhere behind her. Veronica had no idea where.

She turned right. Water, or something liquid, dripped from a black pipe that ran high along the wall. The pipe was as wide as her thigh.

She stopped to examine a loop of wire that had fallen out of place. The dust caked on it could have pulled it down, but the insulation was good enough. She couldn't add this to Greg Collins's list of citations.

Such a shame.

Veronica reached another turn. The corridor, with its hanging loops of wire, continued, seemingly never-ending.

Water dripped. Somewhere in the building, a door clanged shut.

Splash.

Three of the fluorescent tubes here were blown out, leaving just pairs of glowing orange tips, so she didn't notice the pool of water on the floor until the hem of her trousers was wet.

"Dammit."

She shook her foot and hoped it was only water soaking through her shoes.

A hallway opened on her right. *Straight or turn?* Veronica sighed. Collins could tell her how to get out of here, but she'd be damned if she'd go back and ask.

She walked on. The fluorescent light flickered then extinguished itself, plunging the corridor into darkness. Somewhere in the building, the wheels of an old trolley squeaked.

More footsteps echoed behind her.

Finding the wall with her fingertips, she kept moving.

When the footsteps sounded closer, Veronica slowed. They came closer still, faster, heavier.

What the heck?

Veronica pushed herself against the wall, trying to get out of the way of the person who seemed to be running blind behind her.

Splash.

"Hey!" Veronica didn't like the tremble in her voice.

The fluorescent tube flickered on, revealing a hand that held a metal pipe. Then all the colors of the world flashed behind her eyes before the pain in her head dimmed the lights to black.

8

The security room at Pelham Sheriff's Office was well maintained but cramped, in Stella's opinion. A large corkboard covered one wall but held only a pattern of different-colored tacks spelling *Hello* and a small schedule pinned crookedly to the bottom-right corner.

A metal filing cabinet stood next to the door, streaks of rust decorating one edge. Most of the space was dominated by a large desk with two wide monitors, a plastic in-tray filled with dust-covered files, and three empty paper cups, one of which had fallen onto its side to reveal the sticky remains of days-old coffee.

Once Sheriff Marlowe had told Stella about the threat, there'd been a mad scramble to get to Slade's office first.

Ander had been at a slight advantage since he'd stood behind her chair as she spoke with the sheriff. But Stella hooked her foot around his ankle as he moved to Slade's door, causing him to stumble. It'd been Chloe, however, who'd pressed the small advantage, pushing past Stella. Not to be outdone, Stella shouldered Chloe aside, momentarily forgetting about her sling. Chloe had yelped and stepped sideways, giving Stella a clear shot to Slade's door.

She wasn't *proud* of her behavior.

Slade had stared at her, then at Ander and Chloe as they hustled in. Then he'd sighed deeply, as though someone had told him he needed to look for a lost cat just as he was about to capture the Zodiac Killer. But there had been something else there, something beyond frustration at his team's efforts to avoid paperwork and waste resources to chase down a mere vandal. The nod he'd given to Stella's request had been firm and certain.

He told her to take Mac, despite the dark look Chloe shot him. And, further ignoring Chloe's request to go into the field, Slade told Ander to grab Hagen and talk to the fire department.

On her way out, Stella watched as Chloe stabbed her keyboard with that angry pointer finger.

At the moment, Sheriff Marlowe sat in front of the monitors. He appeared to be in his early forties and, with the thin line of graying hair around his head, no one would ever think him younger. His large belly stretched his shirt and pushed him half-an-arm's length away from the desk.

Stella perched on the edge of a chair against the wall, her elbows resting on her knees.

Mac stood behind the sheriff's shoulder. On the desk, a monitor showed footage from around the building. She pointed to a frame at the top of the screen. Her face was stern, her pale eyebrows drawn together in a sharp V over her pert nose.

"Roll that one back."

The sheriff pushed a button on the keyboard.

Mac huffed. "No, dammit. The other way."

Stella suppressed a smile. Mac usually looked like she'd just rolled out of her college dorm into an internship in law enforcement. Her days were generally spent behind her desk, searching databases and sifting through results. The last case, though, the cheerleaders, had seen the entire team dragged out into the field. Slade had sent Martin and Caleb to stake out schools. Dani, who was in her last month of pregnancy, had helped during interviews.

And Mac had been teamed with Stella.

It was the first time they'd worked in the field together, and Mac had seemed out of place, proving she was more comfortable coaxing information out of machines than people. She appeared stronger here. In this room, her gaze was fixed on a couple of computer screens, her face serious.

Sheriff Marlowe tilted back in his chair. "Young lady, I suggest you watch your tongue. Some of us have better things to do than fiddle around with computers all day. If I could spare someone, I'd be doing proper police work instead of—"

"Stop! There. Hold that frame."

Stella pushed out of the chair and approached the desk. "What have you got?"

"Looks like the same guy to me."

Stella studied the screen. Security cameras could be so useless sometimes, even in places where they were most needed. The lens bent faces out of shape. Dirt obscured features. Images could be heavily pixelated. Strange angles hid the information needed most.

This camera had all those problems. The sidewalk outside the sheriff's office curled toward the corner. A long, gray splotch covered the right side of the lens. The person striding away from the building's front door had his head down and his cap low, hiding his face entirely. And he might've had a backpack slung over a shoulder. It sort of looked like it.

But Stella knew. That was the guy she'd seen on the security footage at the resident office. She might not know who he was—yet—but they were clearly dealing with one person. She was sure that when Hagen and Ander reached the fire station, they'd get the same result there too.

"Looks like him to me too."

Mac pulled out her phone and dialed. Even across the room, Stella heard the irritated growl of their injured coworker, but Mac didn't seem to care. "Chloe, can you check the towers around Pelham Sheriff's Office for me? Around…" She read the time stamp at the corner of the screen. "Six ten this morning. Compare the phone numbers there with the numbers we saw near the Resident Agency."

That was good thinking. If the same number came up twice, they'd have a pretty strong lead. Whether they had a serious crime was a different question, but at least they'd have something to follow up if they needed to.

Seconds ticked past. Mac lowered the phone beneath her chin and peered over her shoulder at Stella. "She's checking."

Stella nodded. Her investigative skills were up to that challenge.

Mac pulled the phone back up. "Right. Okay…thanks."

She hung up and shook her head. "A preliminary search doesn't show matching numbers. He might've had his phone off or didn't carry it with him. I'll check again when we get back. But at the moment, there's no match."

Sheriff Marlowe tapped the monitor. "That's a smart cookie, that is. And we've still had nothing from Carlos's phone."

Stella pushed her hands into her pockets. "Yeah. That's some possible premeditation for someone just posting stupid notes on office doors." She took a deep breath. "Have you noticed anything unusual around here the last few days, Sheriff? Someone hanging around more than usual?"

Marlowe ran a hand over his bald pate. "Nope. Everything's the same as always. Though, frankly, a pterodactyl could land on the roof, build a nest, and lay a dozen eggs, and we're so short-staffed we'd barely notice. We've been doing the rounds with applicants but can't find anyone qualified, to be honest."

Stella rested her back against the corkboard and smiled. If she had a buck for every time a cop complained about short staffing, she'd have enough bucks to retire.

"Tell me about Carlos Guerrero. He ever disappeared before?"

Sheriff Marlowe shook his head. "Uh-uh. Carlos is as reliable as my old Chevy. Never had a day of trouble with either of them. Look, he's not the kind of guy who'll make waves or become chief of police. But he does his job, and I can depend on him to do it."

"Have you put out a BOLO for his cruiser?"

"One of the first things we did. As soon as I hear, you'll hear."

"What about his home life? Does he talk to you about it?"

Sheriff Marlowe shrugged his heavy shoulders. "Never *stops* talking about it. Got married last year, and they're already expecting their first kid. He's thrilled. If I hear one more word about the color he's painted their nursery and the price of diapers…" Sheriff Marlowe stopped and ran a hand over his stubbled cheek. "Actually, I'd quite like to hear him complain about that stuff now."

Stella's heart squeezed. The sheriff's worry deepened her own.

She nodded at Mac. "Let's go talk to his wife."

9

Hagen cursed as Ander strolled through a puddle toward the Pelham Fire Station, the water splashing around his soles. Two firefighters in cargo pants and tight-fitting, blue t-shirts washed down a truck. Foam sprayed off the side of the wheels and ran in a river toward the road.

Hagen stepped more delicately. Bubbles rolled past him and slipped down the drain, narrowly missing the toes of his brown leather Oxfords.

Ander stopped, noticing Hagen's careful steps. Then he looked down at Hagen's shoes. "Those Italian things melt in water?"

Hagen rocked back on his heels. These Italian *things* were two of the most expensive things he owned, and he'd owned them for more than a decade. If he took care of them, kept them clean and away from foamy detergents, they'd last him decades more.

Ander, who seemed to prefer purchasing the same off-brand, fifty-dollar work boots every other year, wouldn't understand.

He waited for a line of froth to float past before following Ander. "Almost."

One of the firefighters lowered the hose as Ander approached. Ander pulled out his badge. "Special Agent Ander Bennett. Mick around?"

"Yeah, he's in there."

Ander threw up a thumb and strode on.

The firefighter opened the water again, sending another wave of foam rolling across the driveway toward Hagen's shoes. He lengthened his stride and caught up with Ander. They passed around the back of the fire truck, which was safe, dry ground.

"How'd you meet your firefighter friend?"

Ander shrugged. "It's Kelsey's doing." There was no hint of bitterness when Ander mentioned his ex. "When we were still together, she'd go to this pilates class in East Nasty. Mick's wife used to go there too, back when they lived in town, and the two of them bonded over…" He lifted a shoulder. "Over us, I guess."

As they entered the fire station, the afternoon sun gave way to dark shadow. A second fire truck stood in its bay, ready to rush out and throw water over a house fire or help a cat out of a tree. One wall was lined with doorless lockers, housing bulky brown jackets with fluorescent-yellow trim and numbered helmets waiting for their owners.

Hagen strolled next to Ander, an arm brushing against the shoulders of the heavy jackets. "Pretty sure they found something to talk about that wasn't you."

"That's impossible." Ander grinned. "I dunno. Kelsey used to say she liked having someone to talk to about the dangers of our jobs, someone who wasn't married to the FBI but still understood. I think it was the same for Sheila."

"Who does Sheila talk to now that Kelsey's up north?"

"The wives of other firefighters, I guess. But she's always

on the lookout for a new friend. Every time I see them, she tries to set me up with someone she knows." Ander's grin grew wider. "I could put in a word for you if you want. Just because one of them didn't come up to *my* standards doesn't mean she wouldn't do it for you."

Hagen lifted his eyebrows. "You're offering me the phone numbers of the women who've turned you down? I'm flattered. Really. And I'd love to take you up on that offer, but I think my phone can only hold fifty thousand contacts."

Ander's mouth popped open.

Hagen lifted his hand. "Seriously. No. I'm fine. I don't need your friend's help to find a date."

Ander's expression turned serious. "Is that because you and Stella are getting...kinda close?"

Hagen thought before he answered. There'd been a touch of hesitancy in Ander's voice and far too much gravity. He was more used to Ander mocking him whenever they talked about dates. His question wanted a real answer, as though the reply would mean something. Something important.

Hagen's heart quickened. Ander might really be holding a torch for Stella.

He didn't want to hurt his friend and coworker, but all's fair in love and war. Especially in a war against your father's murderer.

And besides, Hagen didn't even know how to begin to answer Ander's question. "Me and the new girl—"

"Woman."

Hagen gave him a look. "*Woman*...are just friends, okay? We work together, and I'm helping her out with something. That's all."

Ander lifted both his hands in the universal sign of *I surrender*.

They continued past the lockers in silence.

From the end of the fire station came the sound of

muffled shouting. "You gotta do better, Lina. That's the third time this month. You want to stay here, you better up your game."

A door slammed, and a young female firefighter strode toward Hagen and Ander. Her cheeks were red, and her eyes watery. She didn't even look at them as she passed.

Ander lowered his chin. "Mick's in."

Hagen watched the young firefighter go. She didn't look big enough to carry the weight of an air tank, let alone lug one up the stairs of a tall building while dragging a giant fire hose. And yet, if she'd come this far, she must have some strength he couldn't see.

She'd need it if she was going to keep getting bawled out like that.

"Your friend sounds charming."

"Mick's a pussycat, really."

The office was at the back of the fire station. A large window opened onto the trucks and the teams.

Ander opened the door without knocking. Mick Ackhurst looked up. He wore a blue, tight-fitting t-shirt that did little to hide his large biceps or the flat pectorals stretching across his chest. His graying hair was clipped short, and he held up a sheet still attached to a clipboard. "Ander, I can't believe you came all the way out here for this BS."

Ander grinned. "It was just an excuse to see you. It's been too long. And the alternative was paperwork."

"I can respect that." The chief stood and extended his hand. Ander slammed his own into it with a slap loud enough to be heard at the other end of the station. "This is my colleague, Special Agent Hagen Yates."

The fire chief placed his hands on his hips. "Two of you, huh? You guys really take this stuff seriously."

Hagen nodded. "We've got reasons. You've still got it?"

"Yeah." Mick reached down to the floor and pulled a wastepaper basket onto the desk, pushing the keyboard to one side. He rummaged through piles of paper, spilling a couple of sheets onto the desktop before he retrieved a crumpled yellow sheet bordered with duct tape.

He placed the yellow paper on the desk and lowered the basket back to the floor. "If I'd have known it was important to you, I would've framed it."

Hagen pulled on a pair of latex gloves and lifted the note. It was almost identical to the one posted on the resident office's door. The same yellow page, the same wide duct tape, and the same capital letters hand-scrawled across the front.

The only difference was the name.

What Are You Afraid Of, Mick Ackhurst?

Hagen dropped the paper into an evidence bag. "What *are* you afraid of, Mick?"

"Me?" Mick glanced over to a wall of pictures. "Losing a team member, like every fire chief. Our recruit screwing up her evaluation. Sheila overcooking the pasta again. Man, I don't know how she manages to do it. Every time."

Ander laughed. "I'll never tell."

"Uh-uh. Don't you dare. It's like eating wet wool."

"Sauce is good."

"She does make a good Bolognese." Mick dropped back into his seat. "I guess you guys want to see the security footage? There's nothing here."

He turned a monitor around and pushed a button. An image showed a broad figure with a hat pushed down low enough to hide their face. They stood directly beneath the lens.

Disappointed, Hagen sank into a chair. "That's all you got?"

"We got him arriving and leaving but nothing clearer than this. I can send it all over if you want."

"Please do. And have you noticed anything suspicious lately? Someone hanging around the station, maybe? Asking questions?"

Mick pulled the monitor back toward him. "Nope. I mean, people come by sometimes with their kids. But nothing unusual. Though, frankly, we're not really on the lookout for strange things. Everyone knows where we are and who we are."

"Right."

Mick leaned back in his seat. "I gotta tell you, guys. I think this is all a load of BS. It's just some asshole trying to make a point. There's always someone who thinks they know our job better than we do. I'm sure you get the same thing."

He turned and frowned.

One of the firefighters who'd been washing the truck was approaching the office. His shirt was wet, and his rubber boots glistened. He poked his head inside.

"Hey, boss, you heard anything from Veronica? She said she was going to stop by after her inspection and she's not answering her phone."

A wave passed through Hagen like slow-moving electricity. He glanced at Ander, whose eyes had widened, then back at Mick.

"Who's Veronica?"

"Someone who used to work here. She was a firefighter, a damn good one. She's a fire inspector now."

Hagen rose to his feet. "Where was her inspection?"

10

Maria Guerrero, Deputy Carlos Guerrero's wife, clutched a tissue to her face. Her other hand grasped her phone, which rested facedown on her belly. When Sheriff Marlowe said Carlos's wife was pregnant, Stella hadn't considered *how* pregnant. Maria was even closer to giving birth than Dani. The due date couldn't be more than days away.

Maybe that was why Carlos was missing. Perhaps her husband got cold feet on the edge of fatherhood and ran off to enjoy his last days of freedom.

Stella hoped so. If that was all it was, he'd be home in a few days, shame-faced and begging for forgiveness. Then the couple could talk through it and work it out. Maybe there was no connection between those notes and the deputy's disappearance.

Maria lowered her tissue. She appeared to be in her late twenties, with black curls that reached past her round shoulders. Her eyes were red, and her face was drawn.

When she let Stella and Mac into the small house in Pelham, relief had brought some color to her cheeks, as though she was sure, with the FBI on the case, her husband would soon be home. As it became clear Stella and Mac had only questions and no answers, the color quickly left. Maria seemed to sink into the corner of the sofa, opposite Stella but entirely alone.

She sniffed and stuffed the tissue into her pocket. "I'm sorry, I'm being rude. Would you like some coffee? Or tea?"

She tried to push herself up, but her hand sank into the sofa and she only managed a slight shuffle toward the edge before Stella stopped her.

"You stay there. I'll make it."

Leaving Mac in the armchair, Stella passed around the sofa into the kitchen. The open floor plan meant that Stella could make the drinks while still asking questions.

Maria relaxed back. "Thank you. The coffee's in the cupboard next to the stove if you want. There's iced tea in the fridge."

"I'll take coffee." Mac lifted her hand from the armchair.

"Iced tea for me, please, Agent Knox."

"Right." Stella filled the coffeemaker with grounds and fresh water and turned it on. The percolator hissed as the water heated. "Maria, when was the last time you heard from Carlos?"

Maria lifted her phone and tapped the screen. "It was two fifteen this morning. He texted to say he was almost done and would be home soon."

"AT TWO FIFTEEN IN THE MORNING?" Stella found a half-empty jug of iced tea in the fridge. She poured two glasses. Iced tea wasn't her usual choice, but most people didn't have hot chocolate packets lying around in the middle of summer. "He didn't mind waking you up then?"

Maria laughed. It was a pleasant sound that seemed to come from somewhere deep inside her, incredibly genuine.

"He knows that I'll wake up around that time to check he's coming home. You never really get used to those night shifts."

Stella came out of the kitchen with two glasses of iced tea. Mac scooted out a couple of coasters before Stella placed the tea on the table. In the kitchen, the machine dribbled out hot coffee into the carafe. Stella glanced at Mac and jerked her head toward the kitchen.

Mac got the message and climbed out of the armchair. "I'll grab my coffee. You sit down."

Stella returned to her place at the end of the sofa. She sipped the iced tea and tried not to wince. She didn't even take her hot chocolate this sweet. The sugar made her teeth tingle.

Maria took a long draught from her own glass before placing it back on the table. Her hand immediately returned to her belly.

Stella smiled. "We have a colleague at work who's in about the same state as you. I think she just wants it over already."

"Amen to that. I don't know who came up with the idea of nine months. Six is plenty." Maria waved a hand. "I hope your boss is letting her take it easy. You don't want to be trying to do too much. Not in this stage and not in this heat."

Heat?

Stella glanced at the air-conditioning unit on the wall. A pair of green digits indicated that the temperature in the room was barely sixty degrees. She wished she'd brought a sweater. Mac returned to her seat, her coffee steaming in her hand.

"Fat chance of that." Mac sipped her hot beverage. She seemed to relish it much more than Stella was enjoying her tea. "We're always short-staffed. Our boss did tell Dani that he'd try to keep her in the office, but sometimes he's got no choice, you know?"

Maria gave an uneasy smile. She turned over her phone, glanced at the screen again, and turned it back. "If my boss made me go into work now, Carlos would be down there giving her a piece of his mind. Wouldn't surprise me if he waited for her on the way home just so he could give her a ticket." She laughed again.

Stella grinned. Maria was relaxing, as much as she could anyway. Complaining about bosses? It brought the world together. "So Carlos texted you at two fifteen, and you've heard nothing since then?"

The sadness returned. "Nothing."

"Has he ever done anything like this before?"

"No. That's why he texts me. He doesn't want me to...to worry." She retrieved her tissue from her pocket and wiped her eyes. "I'm sorry. I'm so sorry. It's just...I know something has happened to him. He'd have come home otherwise. He'd have called. Please, find him. Bring him back to me."

"May I have Carlos's cell phone number and the name of your phone providers?" Mac put her coffee on the table and reached into her pocket for her notebook. "Also, can I have his email and passwords so I can check if there's unusual activity?" She handed Maria the notebook and a pen.

Maria wrote down the information.

Stella set down her tea. "Does he have any medical issues that may have popped up? We can check with hospitals."

Maria shook her head. "I'm sorry."

Stella nodded and stood. She'd come to the house uncertain whether there was a case here. She still wasn't *completely* sure, but her instincts told her something was wrong.

A man might disappear for a last bender just before his wife gave birth. But not after texting that he'd be home soon.

They had work to do.

Mac stood, then jerked two steps back. "Yikes." She almost slammed into Stella, who stopped her with a hand between Mac's shoulder blades.

At first, Stella was confused. Then she saw what had startled Mac.

Halfway between the ceiling and the floor dangled a spider. It wasn't big, no more than half a centimeter, but it swung in the breeze from the air conditioner, its legs splayed as though performing a cartwheel.

Maria set her phone on the arm of the sofa and pushed herself up. She cupped her hand and collected the spider, placing her other hand over the top to prevent it from escaping. She nodded toward the front door.

"Why don't you open the door? I'll let the poor thing go outside."

Mac didn't need to be asked twice. In two strides, she had the door open and was six feet onto the lawn. Maria crouched to release the spider below the porch. It scuttled away.

Maria pushed herself up and wiped her hands on the sides of her trousers. "I don't mind spiders at all. Carlos? He's terrified of them." Her dark eyes widened as she thought of something. "There *is* a medical condition you might want to check, if you're calling hospitals. It's a long shot, but he's allergic to spiders, you see. I think they're the only thing he's scared of."

11

In a fit of panic and desperation, Veronica Trang folded her legs beneath her and arched her back. The movement pressed her head, which felt like it was going to explode, against a hard wooden plank. She froze, praying for the wave of dizziness to stop.

She had to get out of that box. She just had to.

Her ankles, like her wrists, were tightly bound to the point of nearly cutting off her circulation. Her right shoulder touched the bottom of the crate even as her left shoulder rested halfway up the side of the box.

Her brain pounded, as though the pipe that had struck her in the darkness of the Rugz Textiles corridor was still hitting her with the constant rhythm of a stick to a drum. A wave of nausea rolled in her stomach.

She took a deep breath, steeling herself. *Come on. You can do this.*

With a raw scream, she leaned to the left and pushed down with her bound arms. Her right shoulder rose, and her arm jammed against the side of the crate.

Now she was at an angle. It wasn't much of an angle, but

the ceiling of the box was less than a foot from her face. If she could use her shoulders to wedge herself in place and push her upper body just a little higher, maybe she could knock open the lid with her head and climb out.

Veronica's skull throbbed in protest.

But she had to try.

Ready...set...go...

Veronica pushed the side of her foot against the bottom of the crate and twisted as far as she could. Her right shoulder came away from the wall, but before she had a chance to jam it in place, she fell. Her cheek scraped against the box's wooden walls as she hit the floor with a thud.

"Dammit!"

Something sticky touched her temple. She was sweating profusely, but the substance felt thicker than that. She didn't think she'd cut herself in her efforts to escape, but it didn't feel like blood either.

No...not felt. Smelled.

It didn't smell like blood. She'd seen enough at traffic accidents to recognize that scent up close, and this wasn't it.

This was something else, something wet and viscous and pungent.

She didn't want to know what it was.

There were other smells, too, easier to identify. Urine and the acidic odor of vomit. Whoever had been in this crate before had been in an even worse state than she was in now.

Shit. Someone—or some*ones*—had been in this crate before.

Veronica's breathing came in deep gasps, sounding too loud in her head. She forced herself to inhale, long and deep, then exhale, slow and even. When her mind was clearer, she focused on learning what she could about her environment.

What can I hear?

Silence.

There was no noise at all, not the clanging of metal doors she'd heard in the textile factory nor the wasp-like buzzing of the sewing machines. In the distance, she heard a bird's song and the swoosh of leaves blowing with the wind. Somewhere beyond the crate, a hinge creaked slowly back and forth.

The sound reminded her of the haunted houses she'd been so frightened of as a child.

Oh god, I have to get out of here. Please let me get out of here.

Fighting another bout of rising panic, she inspected the crate. It was long and narrow. Once upon a time, it might have been used to hold pipes or perhaps components for a shelving unit, but Veronica couldn't tell and didn't really care. It hadn't been designed to hold a human being, that was for damn sure. Although it was pretty effective at keeping her in place. Squashed onto her side, there was little she could do to try to escape.

Little, but not nothing.

She pushed again with her feet and dragged her shoulder up the side. Again, she found herself wedged halfway up, the lid of the crate almost within reach.

One more push and—

Down she went again.

Hot tears stuck to whatever else was on her cheeks, making her face even stickier.

It had been a long time since Veronica had cried like this. A road accident on Route 24. An SUV had swerved across the lanes and struck a semi head-on. The truck driver survived. He'd slammed the brakes, shunting the SUV back in the direction it had come. But everyone in the SUV was dead by the time the firefighters arrived to cut them out.

Two adults in the front and two children in the back.

The airbags had deployed, hanging like limp balloons. The hood had crumpled until it was the same height as the vehicle's roof. Trickles of blood on the corners of the children's lips served as evidence of internal injuries.

When they had cut the supports and peeled back the roof, there they all sat, an entire family instantly flung from life to death. The little girl in the back seat—she couldn't have been more than six—had clutched a toy rabbit wedged under her seat belt.

They'd lifted them out one by one, and when they were finished, Veronica crouched on the side of the road and bawled her eyes out. It was the first time she'd wondered whether the life of a firefighter was for her.

She hadn't cried since. Hadn't even come close since she'd shifted to fire inspections. But the tears flowed now.

"Let me out. Please let me out."

More silence.

Veronica stretched her legs as far as she could. Her spine released three quick snaps, none of which helped to ease the pain in her muscles or the ache in her head. She couldn't put up with the pounding pain much longer.

She tried to think.

Focus. You made the inspection at midafternoon. Around two thirty.

She remembered that. That inspection had been the last of the day. She'd planned to stop by the station, type everything up, hand in the citations, and call it a day. Her last memory was of the factory corridor, which was dark. But outside was a bright, sunny day.

At the moment, strips of yellow light shone through the cracks between weathered boards, which meant that night hadn't fallen. Though whether it was the same day, she couldn't say.

She closed her eyes and forced her muscles to relax. She would escape this prison.

Ready...set...go...

For the next minutes or hours, she tried her best to escape. She was a wringing mess of sweat, tears, and blood when she finally collapsed back onto the floor, her strength zapped, her voice hoarse from screaming.

There was nothing she could do. She couldn't get out. There was no one there, and she ached so much. The crate seemed to float away from her, and she floated away with it.

No! Focus.

If Greg Collins, the factory owner, had put her in here, he had to be insane. For Christ's sake, fixing that fuse box wouldn't cost more than a few hundred bucks. It would take thousands to fix the sprinkler system and other infrastructure offenses. Who risked kidnapping for two thousand bucks?

No, he couldn't have done this.

Veronica refused to let herself believe someone would assault and kidnap her just to avoid replacing a damn fuse box and cleaning up his factory floor.

The tears came faster and heavier. "Let me out!" she screamed again, throwing her body from side to side. Immediately, the world tilted. The crate rocked with her movements even more than it had before.

That's it!

Renewed strength flooded into her muscles, and she repeated the same movement. Over and over and over until, finally…

Crash.

The crate fell onto its side. Veronica landed on her torso. Her nose squashed against the box's side. To her intense joy, the lid fell open, revealing a straw-covered earthen floor. Fresh air struck Veronica's face, whipping away the smell of urine and vomit and Christ-knew-what-else that was in there.

She was free. She could get out. All she had to do was

wiggle her body, and she'd get away from the crate, away from this place. Hope poured through her, as vital and refreshing as a cold shower on a hot day.

Footsteps.

They came from outside somewhere. Running.

Veronica moved faster. One shoulder was out of the box. Her head.

How sweet the floor smelled compared to that damn wood.

Forget the smell, move!

She shifted her hip over the edge of the crate. Half her body was outside now. She just had to roll out, find something sharp to cut the duct tape, and she'd be out of there. She'd run and run and keep running until she was safe.

Bam.

Light flooded the room as a barn door was flung open. A huge, dark shadow filled the doorway.

"Help me," Veronica pleaded. "Let me go."

The figure ran toward her. In one movement, he bent down and heaved up the box, sending Veronica sliding back into it. Her heart sank even deeper.

"Nooo. Please."

Her captor hovered over her, a black shape against the afternoon light.

"Veronica Trang." The voice was deep, masculine.

"Yes." Veronica tried to strengthen her voice. "Please. Please let me go."

"Sure." The figure chuckled. "Just tell me what you're afraid of."

12

"I'm telling you, man, that bitch was just trying to put the squeeze on me."

Greg Collins sat behind his desk at Rugz Textiles, his arms folded on a pile of creased order sheets.

Hagen rested his back against the office door. Through the glass wall, a dozen rows of sewing machines clicked and whirred on the factory floor. Each row held about five seats, every spot containing a woman whose head was bent over her machine with no plans of looking up until five o'clock, if that.

Three large fans turned lazily from long poles attached to the ceiling twenty feet up. Their blades barely disturbed the cobwebs between the blades and did nothing to move the air or dry the sweat collecting on the workers' brows.

Hagen glared at the factory owner. He shifted to block the cool flow from the portable air-conditioning unit in the corner of the office.

Collins should suffer too, at least a little.

"Is that right? You think the fire inspector was trying to blackmail you?"

Killer Memo   73

Collins turned to Ander, who sat in the chair before his desk. "I'm telling you guys, that's all it was." His voice rose, pleading to be believed. "Trust me. She was gonna rock up here first thing Monday morning with her hand out, promising to make all my troubles go away." Collins leaned back in his chair, self-satisfied. The chair creaked under the weight of his lies. "Good to see you guys investigating her. About time someone did something about these assholes. These inspectors are all the same. Like I haven't got enough problems."

Hagen wandered forward and rested his arm on the shelf running along the office wall. He lifted the first of five silver balls of a Newton's Cradle that was sitting on the shelf. Then he let it swing. The ball crashed into the remaining four, sending the last swinging away and back, knocking into the fourth ball. A series of rhythmic clicks was bittersweet as he remembered playing with the one that sat on his father's desk so long ago.

Momentum. One thing led to another. One note to another note to another note. Three notes to a missing deputy. A missing deputy to a missing fire inspector. A missing fire inspector to—

Click-click-click.

Hagen closed his hand over the metal spheres. The wire bent between his fingers.

"You got problems, Greg?"

"Have I got problems?" Collins waved a heavy arm past Ander toward the office window. "I've got sixty girls out there and ain't one worth a damn. Almost five on a Friday evening, and I'm still sitting here waiting for them to meet their damn quota."

Ander didn't turn around to check the state of the women and their whirring sewing machines. He kept his eyes on Collins. "You've also got a blocked fire exit. I can see that and

I'm not even a fire inspector. Christ knows what other issues you've got hidden away back there."

Collins blanched. "Now, hang on just one—"

Hagen stepped forward. "We're not here investigating Veronica Trang's behavior. As far as I know, she's on the level, and if she found violations, you'd better deal with them."

He glanced over his shoulder at the factory floor. The only windows facing outdoors ran in a thin strip just below the high ceiling. All were closed, and the glass was covered in grime. The women sat with their backs against the sewing machine behind them. If there was a fire here, no one would get out in time.

"Frankly, Mr. Collins, if I were you, I'd be grateful she didn't shut you down."

Collins gripped the edge of his desk. Color rose to his cheeks. "Shut me...do you know how much money I've put into this place?"

Hagen shrugged. "I dunno. By the looks of it, I'd say about fifty bucks, and you wasted thirty of it on an air conditioner for yourself."

He'd only been talking to this guy for ten minutes and Collins was already getting under his skin. Something about the factory owner reminded him of his dad's old clients. They'd rake in the cash and throw it away on expensive cars and giant cigars while the dealers and the streetwalkers funding their lifestyles lived in hovels and died of diseases they couldn't afford to treat. Greg Collins might be *just* on the right side of the law, but he was cut from the same ragged cloth.

Ander shifted in his seat. Orange foam protruding from a hole in the back dusted his shoulder. "What happened after Veronica Trang gave you her citation?"

Collins's expression relaxed. His red cheeks faded into a

lighter shade of pink as he ignored Hagen and gave his attention to Ander. "Nothing happened. She showed me what she thought was wrong, we discussed it, and then she went on her merry way. No doubt off to find some other victim, grind another decent, hardworking American into the dust."

Hagen snorted. "Yeah, I guess you'd know what it's like to grind decent, hardworking people into the dust."

Ander stood and put himself between Hagen and Collins. "Did you see her leave?"

Collins frowned. "The building? No. It's a big place here. I didn't take her by the arm and show her out. The less I saw of her, the better."

"You got any security cameras?"

"Sure, plenty. Well, none that work. They were here when I took over the place, and I never saw a reason to pay someone to fix them. What's someone gonna steal in here?" Collins waved his hands around the grubby office.

Hagen rolled one of the Newton's Cradle balls between his fingers. "So, as far as you know, Veronica Trang came here, conducted her inspection, showed you what you needed to fix, and left. Is that right?"

Collins pushed to his feet, clearly ready to dismiss them. "That's exactly right, Agent. Now, if you don't mind, I'm a very busy man and I think I've answered enough of your damn foolish questions."

He strode toward the door and pulled it open, forcing Hagen to step deeper into the office to make room. Ander followed the lumbering man to the door. "Thank you for your time."

Collins patted Ander twice on the back as he held the door open. "No problem. I've always been a strong supporter of law enforcement. I know how hard you guys have it out there, standing alongside your brothers on the thin blue line."

His fingers gripped Ander's shoulder. Collins lowered his

voice and drew his face close to Ander's ear, though his voice didn't lower. "Hey, listen. I also know you guys don't get paid enough. You two want to stop by every now and then, I'd be happy to put a few gifts your way. Nothing extravagant. Nothing traceable. Just something to help a little with your retirement."

Hagen clenched his jaw. Collins was the kind of lowlife Hagen hated dealing with. Men who tried to game the system—thinking everything was theirs for the taking—pissed him right off.

Greg Collins, who stood with his back to Hagen, didn't notice the anger curling Hagen's hands into fists. "And if you could see your way clear to helping me out occasionally. Getting rid of this dumbass fire inspection report, for example. Or giving me a heads up if ICE plans to conduct another one of their raids. Well, I'd be much obliged."

Ander turned and towered over Collins. "You know, I'm gonna do you a favor. I'm going to forget you said that."

Collins laughed. "Now, come on, Agent. If you don't need the cash, there are...other things I can do for you." Collins nodded to the picture window facing the factory floor. "You just take a look out there. Sixty girls out there, all fine girls. And they're so desperate, they'll do anything for me. You just take your pick, and I'll arrange—"

Hagen was done with this bullshit.

Before he knew he was moving, Hagen had the bastard shoved against the office window so hard the frame shook. His forearm pinned Collins to the glass.

"You'll arrange what, huh?" Hagen leaned close enough to smell the asshole's sweat. "What are you going to arrange, *Greg*, that won't have my sisters on the thin blue line coming round here and kicking your ass into jail?"

Eyes wide with fear, Collins's mouth opened and closed like a fish. "I-I..."

"Scum like you make me sick." His right hand itched for contact. "You think you can buy your way out of anything? Do whatever the hell you want?"

Ander's hand landed on his arm. "Hagen, that'll do."

No, it won't.

The hand tightened enough to pull Hagen back from the brink of doing something he couldn't take back.

Forcing his expression into a blank mask, Hagen took a single step back. "You think some fire code issues make for a bad day? Say another word about those women out there and you'll find out what bad is. Hear me?"

Collins blinked as a bead of sweat dropped into his eye. "Y-you c-can't threaten me." The words were as limp as the man's dick.

"Yeah? Rather I arrest you for offering a bribe to an officer of the law? I can do that. Gladly."

And if I wasn't so worried about Veronica Trang, I would.

Collins held up his hands, a bit of his bluster returning. "I've got lawyers."

Ander pushed himself between the pair. "Good for you. Call them and ask what'll happen if you don't fix your fire issues."

He held the door open and waited for Hagen to leave first. Hagen strode past him. The women watched him as they passed, the sewing machines no longer buzzing.

The agents walked off the floor and into the dark corridor leading to the exit. They were greeted with puddles of dirty water and flashing fluorescent tubes.

Ander closed the factory door and confronted Hagen. "What the hell was that all about?"

Hagen took a deep breath. He'd overdone it. He knew he had. "Sorry. Guys like that, though. Christ, they make me sick."

"Yeah, well, if you hadn't lost your shit, we might've been

able to do something. We bring him in for attempted bribery now, and he'll bring you up for assault. That was stupid, man. Really dumb."

Hagen closed his eyes for a second. Ander was right. He'd screwed up. Not that it mattered. Even if they had brought him in for attempted bribery, Collins might've gotten a fine, but more likely, the case would've been thrown out. They didn't have enough to file charges.

He walked on. "Yeah, yeah. I've just been on edge a bit lately."

Ander caught up. "Listen, I—"

Hagen held up a hand, stopping Ander before his friend could ask if there was anything he wanted to talk about. "Anyway, we didn't learn much about Veronica Trang. You believe she just left here like he said?"

"She might have. I can't see a reason to think otherwise."

They reached a junction.

"Which way?" To the left and right, the corridors were eerily similar.

He could practically hear Ander shrug behind him. "Six of one, half a dozen of the other, I guess. Maybe Trang is still here, trapped in the maze of fire-hazard tunnels."

"Right it is." They walked on in the darkness. Hagen's foot splashed into a puddle. "Dammit."

Ander laughed, pulling out his phone to use the flashlight. A bright, white beam flowed over Hagen's shoulder, casting a giant shadow along the corridor. "I'm telling you, man. Those are not the right shoes for this kind of work."

"They would be if I could see where the hell I was going."

He reached into his pocket and pulled out his pen light. The yellowish glow landed on the puddle of water—or whatever—in front of him. The pool reached almost from one wall to the other. Drips fell steadily from a black pipe attached to the corner of the ceiling. Another corridor opened to the left, half a dozen yards farther up.

"What the hell's that?"

Ander shifted his light over Hagen's shoulder. "Where?"

A clipboard containing inspection sheets and citations sat next to a trickle of water. Veronica Trang's badge lay neatly on top of the paperwork.

Beyond the water, a metal pipe, the size of a baseball bat, rested on the ground next to the junction.

On one end of the pipe pooled a small puddle of dark red blood.

13

The light struck Stella first. Unnaturally bright, it leaked from a passage off the under-lit corridor. The glare turned the concrete walls a bright gray and cast a silver sheen over the wet floor. Compared to the early evening sun Stella had left behind at the entrance, the color was dull and lifeless.

"Guess that's them." Mac moved closer to the wall, avoiding the worst of the puddles.

Stella wiped sweat from her brow with the back of her wrist. The place was stifling. The door at the entrance had slammed shut behind them, cutting off any breeze to move the humid air. Her shirt stuck to her back.

"You're getting to be quite the field agent, Mac. Those investigative skills of yours are coming right along."

Even in the shadows, Mac's grin was clear. "Why, thank you. Wish I could say the same about your SQL database searches."

Stella felt for the wall with her fingers. "My squirrelly what?"

Mac's laugh was contagious. "Yeah, exactly."

Stella reached the junction. About five yards down, a pair of lights mounted on tripods lit the wall and the floor so brightly that Stella was pretty sure she could count the rat hairs on the concrete. Beyond the pool of light, darkness continued behind Hagen and Ander, who stood on the other side of the corridor's glowing island.

Stella caught Hagen's eye. He nudged Ander, and the two of them made their way around a white-suited forensic officer crouching over a small crimson puddle.

Hagen peeled off his rubber gloves. "Slade told you to come down here?"

Stella nodded. "Yeah. He said you'd found something. What've you got?"

"That."

A forensic tech stood, a large evidence bag hanging from his fingertips. At the bottom of the bag was some kind of metal bar, about an inch in diameter and two feet in length. The tech pushed past them, continuing back the way Stella and Mac had come. He didn't stop to give an explanation.

Stella watched him go. "What's that?"

Hagen balled the latex gloves in his palms. They squeaked and farted as they released air. "Not sure. Looks like a bit of metal piping. There's all sorts of garbage like that around here. But this one was lying in a puddle of blood."

A sticky, red pool had collected next to the wall. A weight settled in Stella's chest, as though all the fears floating in her head since discovering the memo had coalesced into something solid and real and heavy.

"Know whose blood it is?"

Ander beat Hagen to the answer, but he sounded no more knowledgeable than his friend. "Forensics can't say for sure yet. They're going to run blood type as soon as they can. But there's no word from a fire inspector who was here earlier today. This was her last call. She did an inspection, found a bunch of problems in this hellhole of a sweatshop, and hasn't been heard from since. Veronica Trang."

That heavy lump in her chest grew heavier still. "Any connection to your friend's fire station? The one that got the note?"

Ander nodded. "Exactly. She used to be a firefighter there. Her inspection office is based out of the station."

Stella swore under her breath.

Mac's gaze was still fixed on the bloody puddle. "But her disappearance might not be related to the notes." Even from a distance and in the glare of the scene lights, the blood appeared to be only partially congealed. "I'm guessing handing out fines can piss off the wrong people."

Hagen nodded toward the exit. "Let's get out of here. It's steaming. Forensics can pick up the evidence."

He led Stella and Mac down the corridor.

Ander brought up the rear. He peeled off his gloves with a loud snap. "We spoke to the owner. Nasty piece of work. He insists Veronica Trang left after giving him her citation and he hasn't heard from her since. There are no bloodstains on his clothes, and forensics hasn't had a chance to run potential fingerprints on the pipe."

Hagen spoke over his shoulder, his expensive Italian shoes tapping against the concrete floor. "Sheriff Marlowe has a couple of Spanish speakers talking to the workers back there. It'll take a while to get through all of them, but so far, they're singing the same song. They didn't see anything, didn't hear anything. And they definitely don't want to say anything. They're terrified we'll give their details to ICE."

They reached the entrance. Hagen leaned on the bar of the fire door and pushed. Even at six in the evening, the sunlight was still bright and made Stella blink twice. The outdoor air was fresh on her skin and almost cool compared to the fetid atmosphere inside.

A low concrete wall ran next to the entrance, and Stella crossed to it and sat down. She rested her elbows on her knees. "So we're assuming the blood in that corridor is the missing fire inspector's."

Ander took a perch next to her. "We have her badge and clipboard as obvious clues that it's her, but forensics will run their test too. The hair on the weapon seems to match her description, the blood is fresh, and no one else has been up and down that corridor this afternoon. The factory owner says he had no other visitors. I think we can safely assume it's hers until we know otherwise."

Stella nodded. The weight in her chest deepened into a heavy sadness. The morning's rush to get out of paperwork had proved more taxing than she'd anticipated. Today should've been quiet. She should've been back at the office, enjoying the monotony of filling out forms. Now she was looking at more blood, more victims, more missing persons.

But if she'd ignored the note, if she'd ignored the inherent threats within it, Veronica Trang might not even be suspected missing at this point. She'd done her job, even if it'd been to get out of doing the other, menial part of her job. They weren't ahead of the situation, but they weren't far behind. That had to count for something.

The parking lot didn't seem to hold anything of note. Two forensic team members were poking around Veronica's car, a white sedan. About fifteen other vehicles, including their own cars, were scattered around the lot.

However, there were no cameras and no marks that she could see, which might have given them a clue to the person who had wielded the metal pipe.

Stella rubbed her ear stud.

"Why leave the weapon?" She caught Hagen's eye. "I mean, why not take the weapon and dump it somewhere? It's not the kind of thing we'd find easily."

Mac rocked on her heels. "Maybe they panicked? Hit the fire inspector, then dropped it and ran off? Or maybe they had their hands full carrying her out of the building while also trying to hold the pipe."

Stella shook her head. "Possibly, but I don't think so. Everything has been planned so carefully. The three notes. The names on the notes. And the organizations that received notes are all missing people. Deputy Guerrero from the sheriff's department. The fire inspector from Pelham Fire Station."

"We got a note too. None of us are missing." Mac glanced from one face to the other. "I mean, *I'm* not missing. *You're* not missing." She leaned close to Ander. "Are you missing?"

Ander grinned. "In general, only my pride."

Though she did appreciate the cyber tech's desire for levity, Stella ignored Mac. "It's all so deliberate. I think he's playing with us. He wants us to know what he's doing. He wants us to know that he's taken a cop and he's now got someone from the fire services."

No one spoke.

A breeze blew hot air over the parking lot's tarmac.

"We need to be careful. We need to assume we're next."

14

She didn't tell me what she was afraid of. I didn't expect her to. No one volunteered that kind of information.

I crouched over the crate, my arms resting on the edge.

She was so small in there, curled at the bottom. Her dark eyes focused up at me, unblinking, like a deer staring just a little too long at the headlights rushing toward it. Her pupils were dilated to different sizes, a clear sign of a concussion. The pipe had done a number on her head. Trang hadn't made it any better by tipping the crate over either.

The box wasn't that big, but from my perspective, she could've been at the bottom of a deep well. Her hands and feet were still bound with duct tape, barely. She'd almost managed to wriggle her wrists from the bindings.

But the smell! Man, the stink of that thing. The crate had only been used to store used irrigation pipes and a cowardly deputy. After the deputy, it smelled of piss and vomit. Urine even stained some of the boards. I could've stashed that thing at the other end of the farm, and it still would've stunk up the house. No wonder she wanted to escape so much.

The stink was nothing compared to what was coming.

The thought made me chuckle.

I reached down and ripped the binding from her hands. I might even leave the tape off. Give her a fighting chance.

"What do you want?" Trang's voice was hoarse from yelling and breathing in piss-scented air.

"To see if you're worthy of the uniform you wear. There's a test. If you pass, I'll let you go."

She appeared thoughtful, assessing. I could feel her trying to figure out my own weakness, but her brain was so obviously scrambled, her thought process was as transparent to me as a windowpane. Joke was on her—I didn't have a weakness.

"I'll make you face your worst nightmare, the thing you fear more than anything else in the world. If you can stare it down, if you can look fear in the face and beat it, you'll get to go home."

She sat up. I allowed her to.

"I have a son. I have a husband—"

"Then you have reasons to be brave. Now, are you going to tell me your greatest fear, or do I have to figure it out?"

I adjusted my crouch. Squatting like that was none-too-easy on the knees.

"Look, you seem to have been in the service. Army?"

I frowned at her. What was she getting at?

She offered a small smile, which she probably thought was a comforting expression, but it was out of place against her dilated eyes, giving her a slightly deranged look. "You carry yourself as if you've been through training. You remind me of some of the firefighters I know who've been through the military."

Trang's words brought back the months I'd spent at Fort Jackson, climbing over walls and learning to salute and shoot and crawl through the dirt. The time in Iraq. Wasn't long, but it was more than most, despite what they say.

But it was none of her damn business where I was. This wasn't about me. This was about her, about whether she deserved to wear the uniform I couldn't.

Her hands shifted, reaching out and grasping the edges of the crate. Trang pulled herself straighter. We were face to face. Her straight dark hair created a small static halo around her head. Those dark eyes seemed even more uneven up close.

"I remind you of other firefighters?"

"Yes. The same bearing. Obviously strong."

"You think I could keep up with them? Face down fires?"

"Sure." Her voice wavered a little. She was probably dizzy from sitting up.

I reached into my pocket and pulled out my Zippo. The silver flashed even in the dim lighting. One quick flick and a solid blue-gold flame burst forth.

Trang didn't flinch, but she finally blinked as the light hit her eyes. Her pupils didn't move. Nothing about her moved.

"You used to be a firefighter? You wore the uniform?"

She nodded, her focus now on the flickering fire. "I mean, I didn't wear a ball gown."

I moved the flame closer to her face. "You've seen flames much bigger than this. You've felt heat hotter than this." I held the lighter next to her nose. The tanned skin turned red before my eyes. She blinked hard but stayed perfectly still. An acrid scent filled the air as the fire singed an eyelash.

In a quick move, I snapped the lighter shut.

Trang swallowed hard. "How'd I do?"

I laughed. A deep, deep belly laugh. Right in her face.

She glared at me. Her crooked pupils made her look crazy. If those eyes had been fingers, they would have raked through my eye sockets and torn out my brain. Her fake kindness, her transparent attempts at creating rapport, melted away.

I pushed to my feet. The blood rushed past my knees and made my toes tingle. Made me remember I was alive.

"Oh, that wasn't the test, my dear. You've already told me what you're most afraid of."

In one motion, she jerked the crate sideways, throwing her body weight to the other side, away from me. It was the same move she'd made before. But she underestimated my speed and overestimated her own concussed abilities. I was around the crate in time to meet her staggering to her feet.

A wave of dizziness slammed into her, but I caught her before she fell to the floor.

"How far did you think you'd get?" I glanced from her face to her bound feet, back to her face. She wriggled like a worm for a second, but the fight, while sincere, was ineffective.

"You don't know a damn thing about me. My son is seven years old. My husband and I have been married for eleven years. He hates that I've always put myself in dangerous situations—"

"Enough." I turned her to face the corner of the barn, so she could see what I'd set up for her. "What do you think?"

When Trang saw the arrangement, she bucked like a wild thing in my arms.

I was too strong for her.

Years of physical training paid off.

"It seems I do know a damn thing about you. Let me describe a scene to you. Little Veronica Trang, fourteen years old. Lying in the bath, all nice and warm. You remember that, Veronica? You remember that moment?"

Her mouth opened, her struggling stopped. "How did you know about that?" Her breathing quickened as though she were back in that bath, facing that moment again.

A warmth spread through me.

This was it—this was the moment. When they understood they needed to face their *real* fears.

"You were so comfortable." I stepped around a fallen rake. "Your hair was still wet. You'd just washed it, that beautiful black hair of yours. But you didn't want to get out of the bath to dry it. The water was warm, and the bathroom...well, that was kinda cold, wasn't it?"

Her face turned pale. "How do you...? How...?"

I nodded toward the corner of the barn. An old-fashioned clawfoot tub, deep and heavy, rested there. Cold water filled it to the brim. She bucked harder as I carried her closer to it.

There was a maniacal strength to her movements now.

I *felt* the fear.

She squirmed to get out of my grip but couldn't get purchase.

"What did you do? You stayed in the bath. You reached around to the cupboard under the sink. You took out the hair dryer and you plugged it in. And you tried to dry your hair while you still lay in the bath."

Trang made a strange noise deep in her throat. A tear ran over the bridge of her nose. But she didn't stop kicking her bound legs.

Like a wriggly mermaid.

A wriggly mermaid with sharp fingernails.

One of her free hands, which up to this point had been pushing at my shoulders, reached my cheek. She scratched my skin, almost getting my eye.

I faked dropping her, which served the dual purpose of startling her and allowing me to readjust my grip.

"Man, I've been called dumb in my time but trying to dry your hair with a hair dryer while submersed in water? I mean, that's a whole new level of dumbassery."

She rolled away from my chest, almost out of my cradle grip. But I caught her. Tightened my arms. Almost there.

"Of course, the inevitable happened. Wasn't your fault, I'm sure."

We arrived at the tub.

"Your hands were slippery, so the dryer slipped out of your fingers and fell, the hot air still blowing right into your bath water. Boom! If the circuit breaker hadn't flipped, you'd be toast."

"How...how do you know all this? *How?*"

"Now, what do you think? I'm not some kinda fool. I've done my research, Veronica Trang. I've planned this out real careful. I know everything there is to know about you." I leaned closer. "Maybe don't have such personal conversations in coffee shops where anyone can overhear."

I dropped her in the tub. Waves of cold water jumped along the edges. A particularly large splash hit my face. It felt good. She submerged fully beneath the surface before coming up sputtering.

She scrambled in the water, trying to get a grip on the slippery surface. Her bound ankles made it extra difficult. She reached down to the duct tape, pulling. But between being cramped in the crate and her concussion, she wasn't in control of her body anymore.

I laughed and moved to the steel cabinet where I kept my tools. I'd put something in there recently, all ready for this moment. "How did it feel? A tingling sensation all over your skin? Or maybe it was like an explosion?"

"You don't have to do this. Please...you wanted to save people." She was still trying to get at the tape around her ankles.

"Not weak people! Look at you. Sniveling. Useless. Like back then, right? One minute you're lying there waving that hot air over your head, and the next, a flash of light, a bang, and suddenly, you feel like you're on fire."

I pulled out my old power drill, the cord all torn, the

wiring exposed. The heavy-duty extension cord, already attached to an outlet, just waiting. I picked both items up and plugged the drill in.

Sparks zapped across the exposed wiring.

I lifted the drill and showed her the copper wire under the cable.

Her eyes widened in horror. "No, no. Please no."

I breathed in her fear. What would she do next?

Live or die.

15

The four special agents arrived back at the FBI's Nashville Resident Agency after leaving Rugz Textiles' hell labyrinth. Hagen dragged the chair from under the conference table and dropped into the seat opposite Dani. Stella sat a couple of places down, sandwiched between Mac and Ander. Hagen had barely had a chance to speak to her all day.

Not that it mattered now. What was supposed to have been an easy slide into the weekend had turned into another case. No one would be going to Atlanta to follow up on Joel Ramirez anytime soon. They would have to wait another week. At least.

Slade strode in and dropped his phone onto the table. His face was taut, the gray bags under his eyes darker and deeper than usual. He hadn't quite recovered from the cheerleading case, which had struck Slade close to home. And now, before even getting a good nap in, another case. Slade glanced at his watch and grimaced before he lifted his face and addressed the room.

"It appears even when we don't have a murder to work

on, cases come looking for us. I've asked every sheriff's office, fire station, police station, and every other government organization within a hundred miles of here to report receiving one of those notes."

Chloe pushed her fingers through her short, black hair with the hand not hampered by her sling. "Did you check the sanitation department?"

Slade paused. He spread his fingers over the end of the table. "That is a fair question, Chloe, and you know what? I did. The good news is that no one else has reported receiving a message on their front door. So it's just us, Pelham Sheriff's Office, and Pelham Fire Station at the moment."

Chloe sat back in her chair. "Maybe we should buy a lottery ticket."

Stella frowned. "Lotteries are random. This guy's deliberate." She turned to Slade. "Is there anything connecting us to the sheriff's office and fire station in Pelham?"

Slade shook his head. "Not as far as I can see. Ander knows the fire chief in Pelham. Any one of you have a connection to the sheriff's office there?"

The room was silent. Hagen's gaze slid from Dani to Chloe and around the table to Ander, Stella, and Mac. No one nodded.

"Yeah, that's what I thought." Slade glanced at his watch again and swore. "I thought this was going to be a quiet day. I've got reservations for seven thirty. Anniversary dinner."

Dani rubbed one hand over her belly. Even with the air-conditioning, a bead of sweat ran down her temple. But she grinned, despite her clear discomfort. "Congratulations, boss. That's awesome. Give my best to Jane."

Chloe flashed a smile. "Your fiftieth, huh? That's gold, isn't it?"

"Very funny. Nineteenth." He lowered his voice as though talking to himself. "It's just the nineteenth."

Dani laughed. "And I'm sure they were the best nineteen years of your life. But let's get you out of here. Otherwise, you won't reach your twentieth."

Slade smiled. "True. For now, we've got the three messages and no clear connection between them. Forensics are working on the notes. The handwriting looks the same, and both the paper and the duct tape appear to come from the same source. Forensics have matched the angles of the cuts on the tape. The notes appear to have been taped one after the other."

Hagen nodded. That was good news. The perp might have posted more notes before or after these three, but if the cuts *hadn't* matched, they'd be looking for more notes and more victims.

Stella leaned forward. "Has the sheriff received any more news regarding Deputy Guerrero?"

"No. Nothing at all. He seems to have vanished. They can't even find his car. Apparently, the GPS system in the cruiser is faulty, and they're so short on people, they haven't been able to fix it. So they don't even know where he went missing."

"That could be hopeful, right?" Dani shifted in her seat. "I mean, we don't *know* something's happened to him. He might've just driven off somewhere."

"Let's hope so." Slade didn't sound convinced. "Sheriff Marlowe has sent someone from the station to stay with his wife. Let's hope Dani's right, and he rolls up soon with a bunch of flowers and a sheepish apology. However, we need to be realistic. His debit card and his credit cards remain inactive."

Hagen blew out a puff of air. That wasn't good news. Humans had needs, and unless Guerrero had a wad of cash, he'd need to spend money soon on food or gas.

"But we do know what happened to Veronica Trang."

Slade waved a manila folder. "Her car was still in the lot at the textile factory, and while the DNA tests will take time, forensics now say the blood found at the factory and on the piece of pipe matches her type. The pipe was wiped, and the assailant must have worn gloves."

Mac ran her fingernails back and forward over the surface of the table. She looked almost disarmed, sitting there at a table with no keyboard or monitor in front of her, like an angler on a riverbank without a fishing rod. "We need to write our congressman about making sure all law enforcement agencies and fire stations have up to date surveillance equipment installed. This is ridiculous. We should have more to go on."

Stella nodded. She propped her elbows on the conference table, looking as empty-handed as Mac. "It's all too clean, isn't it? We've got a little security footage but nothing useful. We've got a weapon but no fingerprints. And we've got no phone network patterns at all. This is someone who knows what they're doing."

Chloe leaned back in her chair, rocking onto the back two legs. If she fell, she'd cost herself another week or two in the sling. "Lucky him. I wish I knew what we were doing."

"Let's clear that up for you right now, Chloe." Slade slipped his phone into his pocket. "The sheriff's office is looking for Carlos Guerrero's cruiser. We can leave that to them." He shot her a look. "Chair on the floor."

After all four legs were safely on solid ground, he turned to Hagen and Ander. "Tomorrow, I want you two to talk to Veronica Trang's husband. See if you can find a link between her and Carlos Guerrero. Stella, Chloe. You two can go back to the sheriff's office. Dig into the deputy's background. See what you can learn about him. There may be stuff there his colleagues just take for granted."

Slade's phone rang. He pulled it back out of his pocket,

glanced at the screen, and lifted a finger as he answered. "Yep…yep. Leaving now."

He dropped the phone back into his pocket and headed toward the door, stopping with his hand on the handle. "Almost forgot. Mac and Dani, be here first thing tomorrow. I want you looking for a link between us and the missing pair."

Opening the door, he stopped again and turned to face the room. "And all of you, stay alert. One person connected to each location has gone missing. I don't want any of you to follow them. Stay safe."

16

Stella sat at her kitchen counter and clutched her phone. She had to do it. She couldn't wait any longer. Her finger hovered above the screen.

And stayed there.

Calling her mom should've been easy, the kind of thing a daughter did because she wanted to, because she had something interesting to share or some advice she needed. A call like this shouldn't have been something Stella had to endure.

But that was her mother. Barbara Fiedler Knox Rotenburg had never supported her decision to join law enforcement, and ever since her mother moved to Florida, all she really wanted to know was when Stella was going to give up her awful career choice and join her. All she spoke about was her friends and her husband, Jonathan.

Stella didn't mind that her mother had managed to find someone after her father died. She was even relieved her mother wasn't alone. But there were also times, late at night, when Stella lay with her arms behind her head, when she was surprised. And a little angry.

The ease with which her mother had turned her back on

their life in Memphis and built something so different. It was as though she had been able to just…cut a cord and float free.

Though, speaking to her mother always reminded her that escape was possible if she wanted it.

Stella groaned. There was no getting around this call. Jonathan had had a heart attack a few days ago. Nothing too serious by the sound of it. More of an incident than an emergency. A reconnaissance more than an attack. But it, of course, scared the daylights out of his wife. Her mother needed some mothering.

In the aquarium next to her, Scoot the goldfish flicked his tail and floated toward her, mouth opening and closing nonstop.

Stella sighed. "Yeah, yeah. It's easy for you. All you do is swim around and exercise your jaw."

The fish didn't move. His tail flapped gently in the water.

Stella rolled her eyes. "Fine. But I'm blaming you."

She jabbed the call button.

The line rang once, twice, three times before Stella's mom answered with her long, "Hellooo?" Her voice rose into a question as though she couldn't possibly know who had called her.

Stella took a deep breath. "Hey, Mom. It's me."

The line was silent for just a second too long. "Oh. Hi, honey. How good of you to call."

"Finally" was deeply implied.

Stella blinked. Only her mom could turn a simple, polite statement into a rebuke.

"I'm just calling to see how Jonathan's doing."

"Oh." The tension in her mother's voice faded. She sounded surprised. Pleasantly surprised, but surprised, nonetheless. "Well, thank you for checking, honey. He's doing better. The doctors said he could come home, so he's here now."

"That's great."

"It *is*. It's good to have him back. The doctor told him he has to take these little pills now, so he's set a reminder on his phone. He's only forgotten once, and I pulled him up on it right away. He has to take care of himself."

"I'm sure you're looking after him."

The phone fell silent for a moment. "Well, what can I do? Jonathan's children are of little help, and my daughter is busy with her life in Nashville. I just have to do what I can."

Guilt was like a wet blanket tossed over her head. "Mom."

"I know, I know. You're very busy."

"It looks like we've got a new case. It's really—"

Bzzzz.

Stella headed toward her door. "Mom, I'm so sorry, but there's someone at the door."

"Can't you—"

"Please tell Jonathan how happy I am that he's better. I'll call you soon, okay? Love you. Bye."

Stella disconnected the call and a new flood of guilt hit her like a slap. Scoot stared at her with his big, black eyes, then turned his head and swam away in disgust. Stella stuck her tongue out at the fish and checked the intercom. The screen showed the top of Mac's white-blond head. Stella buzzed her up.

When she reached the apartment, Mac didn't come in right away. She poked her head around the door and took in the room.

Stella held the door handle. "You can come in, you know. There's no entrance fee."

Mac slipped into the apartment. "Just wanted to make sure I wasn't...disturbing anything."

"What?" Stella closed the door. "What could I possibly be doing that you could disturb?"

Mac grinned and flopped onto the sofa. "I just thought Hagen might've come back."

Stella sat next to her. The sofa was a bright red two-seater Stella had lugged from one college dig to another. If those cushions could talk, they'd have a lot more to tell than the stories of the wine stains still visible on the armrests.

"No. No Hagen tonight. And thank heavens for that."

Mac pulled at a white lock of hair that dropped past her ear. "Really? I thought you liked Hagen coming over."

Stella pulled her legs up onto the sofa. She'd thought before she spoke. It was true. She had liked him coming over. Traveling to Atlanta would have been much harder alone. She wanted to open up to him. She wanted him to open up too, and yet...he didn't. He wouldn't. And she didn't want to explain all that to Mac. Not yet.

"I appreciate his help."

Mac raised her eyebrows but just saying the words aloud had put Stella on firmer ground. She *did* appreciate Hagen's help and his support in this search. She had the strength to confront Joel Ramirez alone, but she'd have even more strength if they faced him together.

Mac grinned. "Appreciate his help, huh? That's a good start, I guess."

Stella ignored the naughty suggestion. Her focus was elsewhere. "Yeah, but I don't know if I can trust him. I mean, I do when we're on a case. We tackle a perp, I know he'll have my back. Just like you and Ander and Chloe and everyone else. But when we're looking into my dad's murder, something in my gut tells me to watch out. Like, he's not really there. Not for me anyway."

Mac curled the lock of hair around her finger, one of her thinking moves. "That's strange. Who do you think he's there for if not for you?"

Stella hesitated. She didn't know whether Hagen had told

Mac about his father's death. Hagen's background wasn't her story to share. "It's just a feeling."

Mac stood and crossed to the kitchen. She opened the fridge and glanced over her shoulder. "Speaking of feelings. You don't mind, do you? I'm starving."

Stella grimaced. "Help yourself...if you can find anything in there."

Mac pulled out a takeout box. She opened the lid, sniffed the contents, and scowled. "Ugh, Korean. I hate Korean food. Not as tasty as Chinese and not as fun as sushi. Like eating Belgian food when you can choose Italian or French."

She pushed the box back and retrieved a bottle of beer. Checking the label, she released a small grunt of satisfaction and held it out to Stella, who shook her head. Mac popped the cap and took a long sip.

She returned to the sofa, bottle in hand. "Usually, I'd tell you to trust your gut, but I don't see the problem here. You can trust Hagen. And you should. Remember, someone *was* following you. You need to be careful."

Stella refused to show any sense of unease. "I will. Plus, another pair of eyes can only be a good thing."

"You don't think this perpetrator is the one that's been stalking you, do you?"

"No," Stella said, a little surprised at herself for dismissing the idea so fast. "Whoever was following me seemed clumsy somehow. Bright lights in hotel windows. Easy to spot in cafés. That kinda thing. Whoever's hunting police officers and firefighters feels more...*deliberate*."

"Yeah, maybe." Mac took another sip of beer.

Stella started to wish she'd taken one of those beers. "And you need to be careful too. It's important no one knows what we're doing. Like we discussed, if the Marshals get wind of it, or the people Joel's hiding from discover what we've found, there'll be hell to pay."

Mac flashed a grin. "Don't worry about me." She took another sip and turned on the sofa until she was facing Stella. "What will you do when you catch him?"

"Catch who?"

"The person responsible for your dad's death. The one who ordered it and organized it. When you've found him, what will you do?"

Stella reached across the sofa for Mac's bottle. She took a mouthful of beer and swallowed slowly, savoring the bitter hops. "I guess I'll bring him to justice. That's what I'll do. It's what we always do, no?"

Mac took the bottle back. She held it to the light and frowned at the little that remained. "And then what?"

Stella shrugged. As she drew closer to confronting Joel, that question seemed to grow larger and larger, a huge decision she'd have to make one day. If all went well. But she wasn't there yet, not by a long shot.

"I'll jump off that bridge when I get to it."

"Hm." Mac didn't look convinced. She poured down the last of the beer. "You know, I am really hungry. The café's still open downstairs, right?"

※

A FEW MINUTES LATER, they were sitting at a sidewalk table. The night air was warm, but a slight breeze kept the heat on the right side of comfortable. The inside sounds of clinking crockery and grinding coffee beans almost overshadowed the noise of light traffic on the road.

At the next table, a couple dipped focaccia into a small bowl of olive oil and balsamic vinegar, their weekend starting with a casual date.

Stella smiled. Maybe that was the life waiting for her after she found her father's killer.

Mac finished thumb-typing a message and slipped her phone back into her bag. "What's up? What's with the happy face?"

The smile fell away. Back to neutral. "Nothing. No happy face."

The waitress arrived with a pasta salad in a bowl that wasn't much smaller than the table. Mac raised her eyebrows. "Whoa, when you suggested sharing, I thought you were just trying to save your dimes. We could drown in this."

"That's not a bad way to go. I've certainly seen worse." Stella reached for her fork and tucked in. It wasn't until she took her first bite that she remembered how little she'd eaten that day. She really should take better care of herself.

Mac was already on her third forkful. "What do you make of these notes? The ones on the doors."

Chewing slowly, Stella sat straighter, as though switching from discussing Hagen to the case eased a burden. She was on home territory here, where she could explore safely.

"It's a strange one. Usually, someone finds a body, then more people go missing. We still don't have even one body. But we do have a couple of missing people."

"Maybe there is no body. And the missing people aren't missing either."

"I hope. But I don't think so."

Mac grinned. "Is your sixth sense telling you that?"

Stella wished. "No. A two-foot pipe and a bloody puddle in a dark corridor are."

A piece of penne dropped from Mac's fork back into the bowl. "Right. I forgot about that. Wish you hadn't reminded me."

"And then there are those notes. Someone's trying to make a point."

Mac loaded up her fork again. "I don't mind telling you those things give me the creeps."

Stella wrapped a hand over her nose for a quick sneeze. "Hey, listen. We're FBI agents, and we can take care of ourselves. That creep makes the mistake of coming for one of us and he'll have made the last mistake of his life."

Mac's smile was shaky, but she lifted her fork again. "I just wish Slade would send Dani home now. She shouldn't be farther than a short hop to a maternity ward, and if we're at risk, then..."

"As soon as this case is cracked, I'm sure Dani will go on leave. I'm guessing she doesn't feel she can leave while there's a threat like this hanging over us."

"Slade should insist she go home now." Mac waved her fork. A piece of yellow pepper flew over the table, landing in front of a pigeon bopping around the sidewalk. Mac didn't notice. "I just hope that when I'm ready for a kid, my boss will be a bit more considerate."

Mac with a family. Stella smiled at that thought. The sight was hard to imagine now. Mac was too young, too energetic, too full of life to stop and look after a houseful of mini-Macs. But why not? One day. Maybe a family life would suit the cyber tech.

Stella was sure, as sure as anyone could be at any moment in time, that family life wasn't for her.

She'd seen too much loss already. A father. A brother. An uncle, or so she thought. To put that much love into someone and know it could be taken in an instant? No. She could face psychopaths and serial killers, terrorists, and drug dealers. But she couldn't face losing someone she loved. Not again.

She pushed the thought out of her head. "Hey, maybe when you're ready for a kid, you'll *be* the boss."

17

Shnnk. Thump. Shnnk. Thump.

Once again, I dug. The repetitive motion soothed me as I found my rhythm. Dark soil piled up to my knees. My jeans were dusty, and salty sweat beaded on my forehead, but the work felt pure. Satisfying.

At least I had the sense to start early. I made it down a few feet by the time the heat began to build. Figured I'd be done and dusted off before noon. I'd skipped getting some shut-eye to stick to my schedule. Being punctual showed discipline.

"It's just another workout," I told myself. My arms and shoulders were grateful. But I'd skipped leg day several days in a row at this point. If I didn't hit the gym soon, I'd look like Johnny Bravo with those skinny stilt legs.

"The other guys'll wonder how I've built up my arms so much without lifting weights."

I leaned on the spade to stretch my lower back.

The scene played out in my imagination as I resumed digging. *I would walk into the gym. They'd look at my arms and be all like, "Hey, you been benching at home?"*

And I'd tell them, "Naw, just been digging graves for the cowards I've killed."

I laughed into the warm breeze. Those gym rats would all turn as white as a line of cocaine. Most of them, anyway. A few would look at me and give me one of them nods. The slow, knowing nod you'd give a guy you respected and kinda admired.

It was a nod you *earned*.

I lifted the spade and slammed the edge back into the earth.

Shhnk. Thump.

Veronica Trang had not earned such a nod. She turned out to be another disappointment, worse than the deputy. She gasped and struggled, trying to get out. But not hard enough.

When the current hit her, her muscles cramped, and she bent in strange places. Trang couldn't quite keep herself above the surface. Her eyes bulged like ping-pong balls and seemed even bigger under the water.

In the end, I wasn't sure whether it was the water or the electricity or the combination of the two that finished her. All I knew was she did not face her biggest fear with courage.

The names she'd called me. Hadn't been called nothing like that since…since I was in basic training, I guess. But that was then. You expected that in basic. And the guys who did it, they'd earned the right to call me stuff like that.

Trang earned nothing. She had no right. None.

Shnnk. Thump. Shnnk. Thump.

I hadn't felt even a flicker of sympathy when I'd finally tossed that old drill in the water.

After she'd chosen death, she'd looked so funny, her hair all sticking to her face and sitting there fully clothed in that bathtub. Funny had turned to scary as her dead eyes came back to life and watched my every movement.

Shnnk. Thump. Shnnk. Thump.

I threw the spade out of the pit. That would do.

Just made me sick. I expected more from someone who used to be a firefighter. If she'd only been braver, she might've been home by now.

What a coward.

I pulled the end of the tarp, watching her still form closely. Her finger twitched, and I almost screamed in surprise. It twitched again, and her hand curled into a fist.

Her eyes popped open. "What are you afraid of?" My bowels loosened when she laughed.

Taking a step away, I lost my balance as the back of my legs connected with the wall of the grave. A hand came down on my shoulder, nails ripping at my skin.

Shrieking in terror, I flailed against the attack. Fingers crumbled in my hand, bones cracking as I fought and fought and…nothing.

Chest heaving as I desperately attempted to draw in air, I stared down at the broken branch in my hand. A laugh that was much closer to a sob than I would've liked burst out of my dry mouth.

I'd been fighting against the limb of a tree. The dead fire inspector was exactly where I'd left her.

Tossing the branch away, I pressed the heels of my hands into my eyes. They burned from my touch and threatened not to open again.

Was I losing my mind?

Shaking the question off, I forced my eyes back open and focused on my task. I wasn't losing anything, I assured myself. Just got a little spooked, was all.

When I pulled on the end of the tarp a second time, I was ashamed of how scared the movement made me. But fingers didn't twitch, and eyes didn't open this time. No laughter or questions.

Instead, her fried, sodden body rolled twice and landed with a thump at the bottom of the shallow grave.

I picked up the spade again.

Maybe those brave folks at the FBI would have more courage.

Maybe I would too.

18

Hagen and Ander arrived at VinMarket, the shop owned by Veronica Trang's husband, first thing in the morning. The smell struck Hagen first. Dry and dusty, with a hint of acrid chili peppers and a touch of old vinegar. He paused in the doorway. Phil Trang's VinMarket was the kind of grocery store he liked best.

Expensive stores on upmarket streets with shelves of vintage wine and strange-colored salt were fine when you wanted to add something special to a recipe. But it was in these little independently owned places, with piles of old boxes and untranslated labels, where you could dig up ingredients to make a dish really sing.

"You going in, or are you going to stand there all day?"

Behind him, Ander sounded more surprised than impatient. His friend wouldn't have understood. The only thing Ander needed to improve any dish was a splodge of extra ketchup.

"Not *all* day. Maybe some of it."

Hagen stepped farther inside. The store was tiny. Open boxes of cardamom, cinnamon, cloves, and about half a dozen different kinds of dried chilis divided the space into two narrow aisles. Noodles lined one shelf, stretching across the full spectrum of types from thin glass noodles, through buckwheat, and all the way to fat ramen—perfect for soups.

At the counter by the door, a young woman stood behind the cash register. Her black hair had been dyed halfway to blond. A stud glinted in her nose as she flashed a smile. "Looking for anything in particular?"

Hagen pulled out his ID. "Phil Trang here?"

The woman blinked hard, as if she wasn't sure the FBI lettering on his badge was real. "He's in the storage room. It's not…it's not bad news, is it?"

"Thanks."

Hagen squeezed up one of the aisles. If he turned around, he was sure he'd see the cashier leaning over the counter, watching them make their way down the aisle. Cans of jackfruit, palm hearts, and straw mushrooms called to him from the shelves. Dropped peppercorns cracked under his feet.

Ander stomped behind him, his shoulders brushing against the sides of spice boxes. "Man, if they get more than three people in here, they'll have a line outside the door."

Hagen peered over his shoulder just in time to see Ander knock over a package of *kimchi* spices. Luckily, Ander caught it before it landed on the tile floor. He placed it back on the shelf. "I don't think they ever get a line out the door."

At the end of the aisle—sandwiched between a freezer that's glass front was coated with ice and a fridge leaning at an unnatural angle—stood a plain, white door. *Employees Only* was stenciled in green paint. Ignoring the sign, Hagen opened the door and entered a room barely bigger than the closet in his bedroom…and far less organized.

Cardboard boxes reached from floor to ceiling. Pallets filled with a dozen different sauces were lined up against one wall. A man stood in the middle of the room, leaning over a box stuffed with tins of preserves. He wore cargo shorts and sandals. A small pot belly stretched his black polo shirt, and he held a clipboard on which he was marking inventory.

Hagen stretched out his ID. "Phil Trang? I'm Hagen Yates of the FBI. This is my colleague, Ander Bennett."

The clipboard shook in Phil Trang's hand. His face paled. "Is she all right? Of course not. Otherwise, you wouldn't be—"

Ander held up a hand. "There's no news. We just wanted to ask you a few questions."

Phil lowered the clipboard onto the packets of preserves and sat on the edge of one of the cardboard boxes piled against the wall. His neck bent, and his shoulders sagged.

Hagen cursed himself. "I'm sorry. I didn't mean to—"

"It's fine." Phil swiped at his forehead with his shoulder. "How can I help?"

Ander pushed past Hagen and found a patch of empty floor between the preserves and a pallet of black vinegar. "Are you sure you want to work right now? I was kind of surprised you were here instead of at home."

Phil shook his head. A lock of black hair bounced on the crown. It didn't seem like he'd bothered to brush it that morning. The state of his hair and the haggard expression on his face suggested he had slept little that night.

"No. I can't stay there anymore. Just thinking. And this place can't run itself. I have orders, customers. There's a lot to do. I left my son with my parents. If there's news, you can find me here."

Hagen might have done the same thing. Sometimes, the only way to find solace was by throwing yourself into work. "Can you tell me if your wife has received any threats recently? If you've noticed anything or anyone suspicious?"

Phil frowned. "Suspicious. What do you mean?"

Ander propped an elbow on a metal shelf. He was clearly

trying to keep the conversation as nonthreatening as he could. "Someone out of place? Someone asking strange or personal questions? Someone who seemed overtly dangerous?"

"Dangerous." Phil almost spat the word out. "Everything Veronica does is dangerous. When we had our son, I told her I didn't want her to fight fires anymore. Too dangerous. Did you know the year my son was born, three firefighters from her station were killed when they flew west to put out those wildfires? Every time she got a call-out, I would sit here or at home and worry. I don't know how those other spouses do it."

"It can be tough for spouses of firefighters. And law enforcement." Ander's voice was quiet. Hagen glanced at him. A ghost of something flickered across his friend's face. Hagen knew this ghost's name. Kelsey. Ander's ex.

Phil Trang looked just as haunted. "You never get used to it. It's constant worry. All the time. I wanted her to come and work with me here in the shop. It's much safer. She'd be much better than the girl out front. That one doesn't even know the difference between *pho* and *canh*."

Ander seemed a little confused and started to say something. Hagen cut him off. "I'll explain later. But Veronica stopped fighting fires, correct?"

"Uh-huh. Becoming a fire inspector was her compromise. She wasn't prepared to waste all her training and she wanted a job with more…meaning. Like selling food isn't important. Okay. Fine. Inspection is safer. I felt better. No fires and smoke. Just a-holes with bad electrical sockets."

Despite the chaotic piles, the electrical outlet halfway up the wall was new, and there was a clear path to the back door. Veronica had clearly had a positive effect.

"Any of those a-holes ever threaten her?"

Phil shrugged. "I don't know. Maybe. I don't think she

would tell me if they did. She's a strong woman. Someone threatens her, and she threatens them right back. She never takes crap from anyone."

Ander crossed his arms, a move that reminded Hagen of Slade when he stood at the front of the briefing room. "You didn't think of joining the fire service yourself? Might've made you feel better if you knew how well they're trained and how seriously they take safety."

Phil shook his head. "No way. Too scary. I'm not running into no burning building. I see a fire, I run away. There's a reason they're called Pelham County's Bravest."

Hagen smiled. He was warming to Phil's honesty. He seemed to know who he was, and he wasn't going to pretend to be something he wasn't. There was some freedom in that attitude.

"So no suspicious people hanging around here. What about fights? Conflicts? Any neighbors get into an argument with you? Or maybe business partners who are upset about something?"

Phil pushed the wild lock of hair back against his head. As soon as he lowered his hand, the lock sprang back up. "We get some racist attacks sometimes. Not many Vietnamese shops around here."

Ander frowned. "Really? You report them?"

"Report them?" Phil let out a bark of laughter. "At first, yeah. No one did anything. Apparently, the sheriff's office is short on staff. That's what they told us. Now, who do we have to report to? The local government or the same short-staffed sheriff's office?" Phil sighed, and it sounded to Hagen like he was heaving the weight of the world out of his lungs. "Anyway, it's nothing serious. An angry customer. Some paint on the shutters. Nothing I can't handle."

Hagen hid another smile. Phil might not be much of a

firefighter, but there was steel in his backbone, even if Phil himself didn't appreciate it.

"When was the last time someone tagged your shutters?"

Phil shrugged. "I don't know. Last time? Maybe eight months ago."

Hagen lifted an eyebrow. Eight months was a long time. Maybe it was something they should look into, but his gut told him racism was an unlikely motive here.

"Still. If it happens again, you should let the police know. Some creep bothers you like that, they should be hauled in."

Phil waved the thought away. "Too much hassle."

Ander lifted a jar of preserves from the box by his knees. He read the label and dropped it back. "And you've heard nothing from Veronica at all since she went missing?"

The edges of Phil's lips turned down. For the first time, there were tears in his eyes. The fear he'd been fighting was much closer to the surface now. "Nothing. Please. Find her. I can't lose her."

Hagen offered a steady gaze, the only comfort he could extend. "We're doing everything we can."

They left him to his organizing.

Phil was doing well at keeping himself busy. But some things even work couldn't bury.

19

The atmosphere at Pelham Sheriff's Office was as tight as an overinflated balloon. One wrong word, one suspect with a sarcastic comment about hurting a deputy, and the place would explode. Carlos Guerrero's colleagues were hoping for a reason to unleash their frustration. Nothing made a law enforcement officer angrier than injury to one of their own.

Stella understood their frustration. She glanced over at Chloe, who slid a finger under her sling to scratch an itch.

After Chloe was shot, the most satisfying moment for Stella was punching the asshole responsible in the face.

Until Carlos Guerrero walked back through the door that Stella now held open for Chloe, jokes were out. No one would discuss a TV show, talk about a ball game, or recommend a great new place to get ribs. All unproductive conversation would draw a sharp look, the kind of silent rebuke impossible to ignore.

And if Carlos didn't walk through that door, if—instead of gathering to hear his story and judge his explanation—the deputies were forced to gather and say their final farewell, the pressure would leak out slowly. Eventually, the only thing left would be memories of Carlos, maybe some funny stories told by the men and women who served with him. Then, one day surprisingly soon, the stories would fade, the cubicles would fill with new men and women who'd only heard of him.

Stella wondered briefly how many officers in the Memphis Police Department remembered her own father.

"You two from the FBI?"

The question came from the deputy on duty. A single flap of black hair fell halfway over her forehead. She came around the desk and stood with her hands on her hips in the station's entrance hall. Even without knowing her name or badge number, Stella understood this deputy knew and cared about Carlos Guerrero.

Stella took a deep breath, steeling herself for frosty greetings, and showed her badge as they approached the woman. She noted her name as she drew closer. "That's right, Deputy Hodges. We're here to go over Deputy Guerrero's files. Personnel, arrest records, stops. Whatever you've got."

Hodges's black eyes fixed on Stella's face, clearly sizing the interloping FBI agent up and determining whether she was worthy of investigating her missing colleague.

Stella didn't flinch. Showing weakness would make things difficult later.

From behind her came the sound of Chloe's voice, impatient and sharp. "Deputy, we're here to help. Are you going to give us access to those files or not? Because right now, you're wasting our time. And we don't have time to waste."

Hodges nodded sharply, accepting this before turning on her heels. "This way."

She led them to a room that also seemed to serve as both

a conference room and a secondary office space where a large desk held two monitors back to back. Two buzzing vending machines lined one wall. A panel of dull windows provided a line of sight to the front entrance and a glimpse into the roll-call space.

The deputy shook the mouse to wake the computer and tapped in a password.

"You can find everything you need right there. I'll tell Deputy Guerrero's partner you're here."

She left them to it.

Chloe dragged over a chair from behind one of the empty desks. She'd really become quite adept one-handed.

Stella made herself comfortable opposite the screen, though she wished for Mac's skills at the moment.

Here she was again, in a sheriff's office, plowing through records. For a moment, the room seemed to expand and grow until it was as wide and broad and busy as the police station where she had served for two years in Nashville.

One officer had died during her tenure there, a twelve-year veteran killed in a car crash while chasing a suspect.

That day, the atmosphere in the station had changed.

Dan Garcia, her former partner, had been like granite. He'd said little at the best of times. He'd said nothing at all at the worst. Some of her former colleagues had been full of anger, keen to tear the city apart brick by brick until they found the drunk fool who'd caused the officer's death. A couple surprised Stella by collapsing into balls of tears, barely able to function, let alone find the perp. They were the biggest, the bravest, and certainly the most loudmouthed officers at the station.

And their sadness had washed over her. She'd seen it all before, but it still hurt. The shock, the denial, the slow aching acceptance. Strangely, for a few weeks, the cloud of mourning that had settled over the station made the place seem more like home than before.

But a *missing* deputy was something else entirely. In this office, hope and doubt mixed with fear and horror to create a bittersweet cocktail.

Chloe pushed the chair next to Stella's. "Start with the most recent stops?"

"Not a bad place to begin for a traffic cop."

Stella opened the file as a deputy entered. He hesitated before continuing toward them, stopping with one hand on the back of the chair opposite.

He was heavyset, with dark hair receding above his temples. His pale skin looked like it had seen too many night shifts. The bags under his eyes were low enough to have developed over the years, though he couldn't have been older than his mid-thirties. He shifted his gaze from Stella to Chloe and back again.

"You two with the FBI, right? Looking for Carlos."

Stella nodded. Her lips set into a joyless smile. "That's right."

The officer extended his hand. "Ezra Forman. Carlos's partner."

His fingers were wet, which she hoped was a sign of good personal habits and not a sign of very bad ones. He shook Chloe's hand, too, and pulled out his chair.

"I gotta tell you, people round here are pretty damn furious about this whole thing."

Stella pushed the monitor to one side. "Anger is a strange reaction. Shock I could understand. What are people angry about?"

Ezra gestured toward the flickering soda vending machine, then indicated a patch of peeling paint on the wall. "Look at this place. The county expects us to patrol the streets, keep the traffic flowing, drag drunks out of bars, and do all the million-and-one things that peace officers do everywhere. But we've got about half the staff we need, an office that's falling apart, and no damn budget."

"That's rough."

"It means I was working a different shift when Carlos disappeared. I keep wondering. If I'd been there..." Ezra sighed.

Chloe rested her good elbow on the table. "Tell me about Carlos. How long have you two been partners?"

"About three years. He's a good dude. Look, he's not the sharpest tool in the box. I'll be surprised if he ever makes sergeant. But he's all right at what he does and he's happy doing it. Not too many people can say that."

Stella pulled out her notebook. "You're saying everything was fine at work?"

Ezra shrugged. "Yeah. I mean he'd probably like more money, less hours, and fewer night shifts, but hey, that's the job, right? Probably the same for you guys."

Chloe laughed. "Yeah, something like that." She patted Stella on the back, maybe a little rougher than necessary, forcing Stella forward about an inch. "She used to be a cop, though. She probably understands more about your shifts than I do."

"Oh, yeah?" Ezra turned his gaze back to Stella and nodded in approval. "So you get it."

Stella gave him a small smile, gritting her teeth against the stinging on her back. That was some smart, if painful, teamwork on Chloe's part, using Stella's background to build a connection with Carlos's partner. It meant they had a better chance of Ezra opening up.

"What about homelife? How are things there?"

Ezra grinned. "He's expecting his first kid. The guy couldn't be more psyched."

Chloe pushed herself out of the chair and crossed to the coffee machine.

Ezra lifted a finger. "I'll take a cappuccino if you're buying."

With her free hand, Chloe rammed a button, then she leaned against the wall. "Guys can get nervous when there's a kid on the way, can't they?"

"Not Carlos. I mean, who knows? But he couldn't wait to become a dad. Wouldn't stop talking about how he was going to take him to a ball game, teach him how to pitch. This isn't baby nerves. Wouldn't be like him at all."

Chloe set one cappuccino and then another on the table. The foam rocked around the edges of the cups without spilling a drop. Yes, she was getting much better at negotiating day-to-day activities with her injury. "What about his wife? Maria. Things good with them?"

"Oh yeah. Those two are like...Jack Daniel's and Memphis ribs. Sometimes you see a couple and you know they were made for each other." He slurped his cappuccino and licked away the foam on his upper lip. "She made the right decision, dumping that loser she was seeing and going out with Carlos instead. They were married...must've been only eight months later."

Stella's fingers drifted toward her ear stud. "Who was she seeing?"

"What *was* his name? Ivor? Igor? Ian?" He shook his head and took another sip. "That's not right. *Ivan*. That's it. Ivan Scheffler. A real meathead. Owns a gym on Montgomery Avenue. He did *not* like losing out to Carlos. Used to call her up and either beg her to come back or threaten her if she didn't. A couple of the guys had to go out there and warn him to tone it down."

A duty officer stepped into the room. "Hey, Ezra. You got a call."

Ezra placed his palm on the table as he rose from the chair. "If you need anything..." He strode away.

Stella twisted the gold stud in her ear, considering this new information. "I think we can stop with the stops for now. I want to talk to Maria."

20

By the time Stella and Chloe pulled up, three other cars were already parked outside the small whitewashed house where Carlos and Maria Guerrero lived.

Chloe lifted her slinged arm, pointing at the Honda Civic in front of them with her elbow. The car's silver body was marred by a series of scratches and a few small dents in the back fender. "That's Mac's car, isn't it?"

Stella nodded. She'd recognize those knocks anywhere. But Mac was supposed to be back at the station. What was she doing here? "Yeah. That girl is to parallel parking what I am to squirrel databases."

Chloe gave her a quizzical look. "Huh?"

Stella cut the engine. "Don't ask. I wouldn't be able to tell you anyway."

The front door of the Guerrero house was ajar. Cold, conditioned air carried the smell of boiling beans through the doorway. Stella knocked twice and pushed the door fully open.

About a half dozen people crowded in the tiny living room. Maria sat at the far end of the sofa. She seemed to have shrunk since the previous afternoon. Her belly still stretched halfway across her thighs, but her back was bent as though she had been carrying a heavy load for far too long.

An older woman sat in a kitchen chair next to her, rubbing Maria's shoulders and talking to her quietly in Spanish. Maria's mother, Stella guessed. Three more women moved from the kitchen to the living room and back again, carrying teacups in and out while cleaning whatever they came across. A uniformed deputy stood out of the way.

None of those people surprised Stella. She'd expected Maria's family would be supportive. As Carlos's absence stretched on, they would continue to circle around, bring food, and try to reassure her.

However, Stella hadn't expected to see Dani at the other end of the sofa. She sat with one hand on her belly, the other hand gripping a glass of ice water. She smiled at Stella and Chloe as they walked in, expressing all the relief of a guest who'd arrived at a party too early and finally spotted someone they knew.

As Stella stepped forward, Maria met her eyes. In that single, lingering look was the hope for good news.

The room froze.

Stella was quick to reassure them. "We don't have any news. Only more questions."

The wave of sorrow that washed over Maria made the mother-to-be tremble. She turned to her mother. *"Estoy bien, Mamá."* *I'm fine, Mama.*

Stella crouched next to Dani, giving the other women time to comfort one another. "What's going on? Where's Mac?"

"She's upstairs. Slade sent her to look through Carlos's computer, see if there are any secret email accounts or contributions to dark web forums, or something."

Chloe peeled away and headed to the stairs. "I'll go check."

Dani scooted closer to Maria, allowing Stella space to sit beside her. She kept her voice low. "Slade thought a pregnant woman might be able to bond better with Maria. We're a club, you know. There's a secret handshake and a special blazer."

"Really?" It was hard not to laugh, but Stella kept her expression neutral. "I hope the blazer's fetching."

Dani groaned and shifted her weight. She might need a crane to help her off the soft sofa. "It doesn't fit. That's why I never wear it. I've hardly been able to get a moment with Maria. Her mom won't leave her side. And if she does, her sisters are in the kitchen cooking. One of them swoops in immediately."

"Right." Stella took a deep breath, steeling herself to break through the family wall. "We need to talk to her about a bad ex. Guess we'll just have to be a bit rude." She leaned over and gently touched Maria's elbow. "Can we borrow you just for a second, Maria? Somewhere quiet?"

Maria retrieved her hand from her mother and pushed unsteadily to her feet. For a moment, as she stretched her legs, she wobbled, prompting Dani to slip her hand under Maria's elbow to support her while Stella grabbed the other arm. Maria smiled and let them help.

A second later, Dani also stood, equally as wobbly. Maria linked her arm with Dani's. A warm wave passed through Stella. This was how things were supposed to be, women supporting each other.

She led Maria out onto the porch and leaned on the railing while Maria and Dani sat on the bench, which was sturdier than the sofa.

Maria fanned her face with her hand. Beads of sweat

formed on her deeply tanned skin at her hairline. Her thick dark hair was swept into a loose ponytail, but it had to feel like a blanket on the poor woman's head. "My god, this heat. Never have a baby in the summer. Your husband gets frisky in winter, you kick him out of bed. He can wait. It won't kill him."

Dani wiped the sweat from under her chin. "She speaks the truth. You listen to her."

Concern marred the pretty woman's face. "Oh, my sister in struggle. You should be inside, no? Stay where it's cool."

Dani patted Maria's knee. "I'm okay. Fresh air is good too. But she's got a point, Stella. Time your baby better than we did."

Stella managed a laugh, though thoughts of having a baby nearly sent her running in a blind panic. "Thanks. I'm single. But I'll bear that in mind."

Maria raised her eyebrows. She looked Stella up and down. "You are? Why? With those eyes and that figure. Tell you what, you go talk to my sister. She has a friend at work. He looks like that...what's his name? The actor. Tom something."

"Hardy?" Dani guessed.

"No. Something else."

"Hiddleston?"

"Who? No." Maria snapped her fingers as it came to her. "Hanks. Tom Hanks. When he was on the island by himself, you know? With the ball? He has a beard almost to his belly button. Very sexy."

Dani gave a thumbs-up. "We should get his number."

"Right." Stella barely managed to stop her middle finger from shooting straight up and changed the subject away from her nonexistent love life. *Why do all the Tom actors have last names that start with H?* She shrugged the thought away. It was time to focus. "Really, I'm fine, though. Thanks, anyway.

But speaking of seeing people, I have to ask you something, Maria."

The smile on Maria's face melted. She grew serious, her lips set.

"When you met Carlos, you were seeing someone else, right?" Stella consulted her notebook. "Ivan Scheffler. When was the last time he contacted you?"

Maria rolled her eyes. "Oh, that *pendejo*. He was really controlling, you know? Where have you been? Why didn't you call? What did that guy say to you? Drove me crazy. And his friends were no better. Bunch of muscle heads. And then I met Carlos, and he was so different. Cute, friendly. Honest. And I could see he trusted me. Always. That was how I knew."

Stella leaned forward. Ivan sounded like a promising lead. "How did Ivan react when you started dating Carlos?"

Maria's face was taut. An arm curled around her belly, as if she could shield her baby from the negative things she needed to say. "He didn't take it well. As soon as I met Carlos in that bar, I dropped Ivan like a bird drops a bad nut. But he would call, you know? Beg me to come back. When I didn't, he got a little, you know…"

Dani rested her hand on top of Maria's in encouragement. The movement seemed so natural. She was going to be a wonderful mother. "He threatened you?"

"I didn't take him seriously. He didn't scare me. I was getting close to a cop, you know? A sheriff's deputy. They straightened him out pretty fast. Since we got married last year, I've heard nothing. Better that way."

Mac and Chloe came out of the house, the screen door slamming behind them. The metallic *bang* startled Maria.

"Sorry." Chloe fiddled with her sling, adjusting and scratching at the material. "We're done."

"Great. Maria, do you have Ivan's contact information?"

"Sure." Maria pulled her phone out from her back pocket, shifting her weight into Dani. For a second, their bellies pressed into each other. "Here you go." Maria pulled up the information and handed her phone to Stella. She wrote down the work number, which Maria had labeled "gym," and the home number.

"I'm done here too. Thanks. You've been a big help." Stella handed Maria her phone back.

Maria extended her hand, but not for the phone. She needed help up. Stella obliged, then Maria took the phone. "You think Ivan might have something to do with this?"

"We just have to consider every possibility. That's all."

"It wouldn't surprise me. He's a jerk." She stopped in the doorway, her brow furrowed in concentration. "But on the other hand, it would surprise me a lot."

She disappeared inside, prompting an outpouring of Spanish from the direction of the kitchen. Chloe took the seat Maria had vacated.

Dani shaded her eyes against the glare from the midmorning sun. "Did you find anything up there?"

Mac shook her head. "The guy's got a cleaner search history than me. Lots of visits to sites about cribs and local schools. Nothing suspicious."

Dani pushed herself up. Stella winced as her knees popped. "We should talk to this Ivan guy."

"That's the ex?"

Chloe stood up too. "Yeah. He's got a gym out on Montgomery Avenue. Stella and I will head over there now."

Dani moved to the end of the porch surprisingly fast. "No, that's all right. Mac and I will go."

Stella moved to head her off. "Hey, we can do it. You need to—"

"I need to get out of here." Her voice lowered to a hiss. "Seriously, Stella. I can hardly exchange a word with Maria.

Sitting in this house with a pregnant woman and a missing husband is giving me the heebie-jeebies. Mac's done, so we can stop by the gym on the way—"

Stella's phone vibrated in her pocket. She pulled it out and glanced at the screen.

Mom.

She sighed. "Sorry, I've got to..."

She took the call and walked around the corner of the house until she was out of earshot. Her mother's voice came through, sharp and fast.

"Oh, Stella. There you are. It's awful. I'm so—"

Stella's heart raced. The distress in her mom's voice sent her back through the years, to her brother's diagnosis, to... she forced her thoughts back.

"What happened?"

"It's Jonathan."

Stella held her breath. Her stepfather's recent heart attack, though mild, had set everyone on edge. Even from a distance, Stella was half expecting the other shoe to drop.

"He went for brunch with his golfing buddies. I told him not to do it. I said it was too soon for that sort of thing. And now he's not back and he's not answering his phone, and I'm so worried."

Stella's heart slowed. It wasn't much after ten in the morning here, so it would be after eleven in Florida. Jonathan was probably enjoying pancakes somewhere and couldn't hear his phone ring. Or he was blocking her mother's calls. "Mom, I'm sure—"

"Can't you do your FBI thing? Track him down or something?"

Seriously?

"Mom, I can't just—"

"Oh, wait. Here he is. Thanks, hon. I'll call you later."

The phone went dead. Stella stared at the screen as if it

would give her insight into her mother's thinking. But no. "Bye, Mom. Love you too."

She walked back around the house to the porch. Dani and Mac were long gone.

Chloe sat on the bench alone. She shrugged at Stella. "Dani threatened to make me babysit if I didn't let her go."

21

The walls of Ivan's Gym on Montgomery Avenue were painted in no-nonsense shades of gray and black. A maze of steel bars and machines for chest extensions, arm curls, squats, and pull-ups lined the main floor. Lines of punching bags took a beating from half a dozen muscled men in high shorts and low-cut tank tops. The place stank of sweat, leather, and testosterone.

Thwack.

The smack of fists on leather made Dani wince. Something about the sound had always set her teeth on edge, even when she was the one doing the smacking.

Two of the men gave their punching bags a reprieve as Mac held open the door and the very pregnant Dani entered. She ignored them and stepped around a barbell that had been left in the middle of an aisle. These gym rats didn't appear to have a mind on safety.

The deeper she walked into the room, the slower the sound of thwacking fists became, and the greater the number of eyes on both of them grew.

At the end of the hall, a weight lifter lay on his back,

benching nearly two hundred pounds. Standing beside the bencher, spotting, stood a man with his hands on his hips. He had his eyes on the women, though. His black hair was combed straight back on top and shaved close at the sides, so that his full beard stopped at the bottom of his ears. He wore tight, black shorts and a black tank top with the word COACH emblazoned across the front in bold, white letters.

He stood there unmoving, his gaze fixed.

Ivan Scheffler. Had to be.

Dani and Mac walked between two lines of men, all of them with arms like piles of inflated balloons and expressions that made Dani wonder if they'd ever spoken to a woman who wasn't their mother.

The *thwacks* stopped. Grunts, which had accompanied each successfully raised weight, fell silent. Only the loud, steady beat of techno music bounced off the walls.

Dani walked slow and steady. The rubber flooring made her footing unsure. Now both men's eyes bore into her—the spotter and the lifter—their gaze heavier than any of the weights they were tossing around.

"One. One. Two. Three. Five—"

"What are you counting?" Dani whispered to Mac.

"Fibonacci sequence. I do it when I'm surrounded by anything that makes me nervous. When I want to take my mind off stuff, basically."

The coach watched them steadily approach, his head cocked to one side, his dark eyes fixed on Dani.

Dani clenched her jaw.

When they were almost to him, the coach addressed them. "I think you two ladies are in the wrong place. Men only."

She raised her eyebrows. "Do I look like I want a workout?"

From somewhere to their right, a man sniggered. "Looks

like someone's given you a good workout already."

A wave of low laughter rippled around the room.

Dani pulled out her ID and shoved it toward the coach.

"Ivan Scheffler?" She spoke loudly so that her voice was clear above the techno beats. "I'm Special Agent Danielle Jameson. This is my colleague, Special Agent Mackenzie Drake. We're from the FBI. We need to talk. Now."

The room fell silent. Only the *boom-boom-boom* of the music thumping off the walls remained. Ivan grunted and walked toward the office that stood down a short hallway behind a line of steel lockers.

As Dani returned her badge to her bag, Mac's fingers touched her back. Dani followed her gaze. One of the men stood next to the wall. With his hands behind him, he slipped a plastic bag into the space behind the lockers.

Dani repressed a smile. "That didn't look suspicious at all."

"I'm pretty sure they wouldn't send in the FBI for some black-market gym candy." Mac chuckled under her breath.

Dani followed Mac into the office, closing the door behind her. Ivan was already in his chair, his hands resting behind his head, his hairy armpits on display.

There was only one other chair, and Dani didn't wait for Ivan to invite her to sit down. As Mac took a position in the corner of the office—sandwiching herself between a small pile of weights and a poster of a man flexed in a rear lat spread—Dani eased into the seat.

"And what can I do for the illustrious ladies of the FBI?"

Dani pulled out her notebook. "Sir, can you tell me the last time you spoke to Maria Guerrero?"

Ivan rolled his eyes, as though just mentioning Maria's name had put something behind them that he was trying to swat away. "I'm not answering any questions about that dumb bitch."

"You'll answer the questions I ask you." She sort of hoped Ivan *was* behind Carlos's disappearance. Seeing this guy locked up would give her something pleasant to think about while she was on maternity leave. "What about her husband, Carlos Guerrero? When was the last time you spoke to him?"

Ivan scrunched up his nose like he'd smelled something nasty. "That little jerk? Never."

"Never, huh?"

"Not in the last six months, at least."

"Can you tell me where you were in the early hours of Friday morning, around two o'clock?"

"At a club with friends."

"What about afterward?"

He winked at her. "Went home."

"Alone?"

Ivan lowered his arms and dropped his hands to his desk. "Yeah, alone. Love 'em and leave 'em, hon. That's me."

Dani laughed aloud. It had been a long time since she'd heard anyone use that line.

Ivan glared at her.

"Really?" Dani held out her hand. "May we have your phone? I'd like to make sure you've had no contact with the Guerreros."

Ivan scowled. "Sure. And while I'm at it, maybe you'd like me to bend over for you too. The hell I'm giving you my phone. Get outta here. Go on."

Dani didn't move. She tapped her notebook with the end of her pen. "How about we do this? You give us your phone, and I don't give a heads-up to narcotics to come down here right now and rip this place apart for illegal steroids and other nasty drugs."

Ivan's face paled. He reached into the pocket of his shorts and pulled out an iPhone. He unlocked it. "I've got nothing to hide."

"Of course you don't."

Mac took the phone and pecked at the screen with a finger. "Don't worry. Your gay porn habit is of no interest to us."

Ivan scowled. "Those are pictures of weight lifters, lady. I own a gym, remember? Not that I've got anything against gay porn. I mean, not for me, of course. But for…you know. Whatever. Your bedroom, your choice. That's what I say."

Mac nodded. "Of course. Maria's phone number isn't in here."

"Told you. You done with that?"

He extended his hand. Mac shook her head and pecked some more. "How come you don't have your ex's phone number in your contact list?"

Ivan leaned back again. "Because I deleted that bitch's number when she married that asshole deputy. Look, I haven't seen Maria in more than a year. What she does now is her business. If she's what you came here to talk to me about, you're wasting your time."

Mac spent several more minutes tapping on the device before pushing it back across the desk. "I've put our office number in there. Her husband's missing. You hear anything, call us."

Dani pushed herself out of the chair and followed Mac out of the office. The gym was filled again with the soft *thwack* of leather taking a beating. The men were back to lifting weights and winning imaginary fights.

As she walked to the exit, small hairs lifted on Dani's neck. One man sat on a weight bench, wiping sweaty hands with a white towel. He was identical to all the other muscle heads in the place. But he followed her and Mac with his eyes. Dani kept him in her periphery as long as she could. He watched them all the way through the gym until they walked out the door into the baking sun.

22

I dragged my phone from my pocket and held down the power button. Carrying a phone on a mission was like traveling with your own little spy. That's what they told us in the field. So I held down the button until the phone beeped and died in my hand.

I might've been tired, but I wasn't stupid. Tossing the device into the glove compartment, I gunned the engine.

Game on.

The silver Honda was about a hundred yards ahead, driving at a steady rate down Montgomery Avenue. Traffic was light, which made the car easy to see. It also made me easy to spot behind them.

Careful now. Watch your speed. Don't get too close. Not until you have to.

I lifted my foot.

Truth was, I couldn't believe my luck.

I'd had plenty of doubts. I wasn't afraid to admit it. I was taking on the full might of the government. The sheriff's office. The fire service. The FBI. These people had time, training, and experience on their side. But I had more ability, more skill, and more courage.

And nothing to lose.

There were certainly moments as I stuck those notes to the doors that I thought I'd be caught. Some alarm would go off somewhere, and a dozen guys with shoulders like linebackers would throw me to the ground and haul my ass off to prison. And there I'd stay, wondering how I could have been so dumb as to try this thing.

In the end, though, luck was just preparation meeting opportunity. I'd prepped. I'd seized opportunity. I needed to prove I wasn't just braver than these government stooges but smarter too. I'd followed the deputy for a week. The fire inspector had taken another week. The FBI group had been more difficult. I'd just decided to follow the one with the sling recently. She'd seen some things, I was sure.

Still, I could let her go. Not one, but two FBI agents had fallen into my lap.

There I was, working out as usual…and in walked an opportunity. Twice.

Walked? One of them could barely waddle.

And she thrust out her FBI badge like she was holding some holy relic, like she could blast the darkness with the light of her golden shield.

I didn't know who the hell she thought she was, waving that thing around. Just trying to rub my nose in it. That's all she was trying to do.

I put my foot down again and closed the distance. My old truck rumbled with pleasure.

Wait. This is a bad idea. You're not ready. They're two trained agents against one.

I lifted my foot. The distance to the Civic stretched away.

Stick to your plan. Prepare. Think. Plan.

I took a deep breath and let the adrenaline drain a little.

I'd had a plan. I was going to hang around near the FBI's office and wait for the woman with the sling to come out. She was physically fit and wore black as if to prove how tough she was. Never did like those women who wanted to body build. Should leave the muscles to the men. But she was tough, the kind of woman who could run a few miles and barely break a sweat.

The plan had been to follow her home at a quarter after nine tonight. Her live-in was always at some art show on the weekends, out late, slacking. I'd found my moment to strike. By my clock, I was eight hours and seven minutes away from *Go Time*!

But there was no need for any of that now.

Two of them had walked into the gym like that, like they owned the place. They deserved everything they got.

I put my foot back on the gas.

"I'll show her. I'll show the pair of them."

At least I'd show one of them. The one with the white-blond hair was small and quiet. Didn't say much, even when they were in the office with Ivan. Pretty sure it was the other one, the older one, who did most of the talking.

FBI agent or not, there wasn't much to her. A little thing like that would barely put up a fight.

Or would she?

That was the question I was itching to find out.

Would she be like the others? Or would she make me proud?

The Honda turned off Montgomery Avenue. I gripped the steering wheel tighter, excitement causing me to grow hard.

Someone was smiling down on me because they turned onto that little road cutting through the meadows outside Pelham. For a good few miles, they'd be on a country lane with few other vehicles.

I couldn't have had a bigger opportunity.

My heart thumped in my chest.

They might put up a fight. They could draw their guns. Maybe they'd spotted me already and were leading me into a trap.

My hands shook on the steering wheel. I rolled down a window to give myself a little air.

"Get a grip on yourself," I shouted, though there was no one to hear. "Show me who you are, dammit!"

The words had the same effect on me they always did, the effect they'd had on me all the way through basic training. From the day I entered Fort Jackson to the day I staggered up the ramp into the transporter, I'd felt the same sensations. My mouth became dry. My arms shook from my shoulders on down, and my stomach made little flipping sensations.

I felt it all again when I climbed into the Humvee, and we left the forward operating base. Training or not, I didn't know what we'd find when we drove out of the gate and past the sandbags. I didn't know what I'd find now either.

But I'd soon learn.

There they were, just fifty yards ahead.

Did they feel me behind them? Feel my eyes on the backs of their heads?

They were taking the scenic route. Would probably add about twenty minutes to their journey, but they'd get to look at meadows and trees instead of the tailpipe of an SUV or the ass-end of a semitruck on the highway.

The road was empty. A small ditch ran along each edge, separating the cars from the fields. Farther down, past the bend, the top of a small copse of elms bent in the breeze, making that nice, gentle *ssshh-ssshh* sound I found so comforting. No wonder they came this way.

Made me smile. They weren't even that far from my farm. Catch them here, and I'd be home and dry in no time at all.

I put my foot down.

23

Dani tapped the screen of the satnav in Mac's car and expanded the map.

"Let me do that. You're driving." Mac leaned over from the passenger seat, but the map was already on-screen.

"Too late."

This was a much better route. Green hills rolled away on either side of the car. The early summer sun had burned the tips of the grass orange, but the elms and poplars dividing the meadows were a lush green. A wire fence ran along the ditches on the side of the road, reminding Dani this land had a use. Farmers brought their cattle into the pasture, left them to eat the sweet grass, and rounded them up again.

The peaceful scenery was relaxing after her gym adventures. Dani was in no rush to get back to the office. She needed a moment to gather her thoughts and driving always helped her do that. It was the reason she'd asked for the keys.

For the last few weeks, as her pregnancy had developed and her mobility declined, Slade had kept her behind a desk. Every day she drove from home to the office, sat in front of a computer screen for eight hours, and then turned around and went home.

Sitting behind a desk and punching a keyboard wasn't why she'd joined the FBI.

She recentered the map. Mac reached forward again, a split second behind. Dani swatted her hand away. "Too late again."

Not that she blamed Slade. He was only looking out for her.

And the desk stuff kept Theo happy too. Her husband had always been proud of her FBI work, but as family life drew closer, the worry on his face had grown more pronounced. Small lines now seemed permanently stamped between his eyebrows. His silence as she excitedly described cases over dinner had become more drawn out too. The cheerleader case had doubly concerned him because she'd been in the field.

He would never ask her to quit or demand she move to a safer position. But she knew what he thought. His concern was written in the way he lowered his head as she discussed a crime scene. It was obvious in the way he picked at his food when she talked about a witness. She'd be on leave soon and she hoped his concerned face would relax a little.

On leave. At home. Alone with the baby for most of the day.

A whole new life. A whole different pace.

The thought sent a shiver through her. She eased up on the gas.

Nothing in all her years in the FBI both excited and frightened her as much as impending motherhood did. She wanted it now, and she also wanted to keep putting the moment off until she was sure she was ready.

Like that's ever going to happen.

She let the car slow and stretched her back.

"Thanks for letting me drive. I've got a feeling that once this baby pops out, I'm not going to be out and about much."

"Pleasure. I'm always happy to ride shotgun. It's like a road trip." Mac turned the dial on the radio. "Ooh, love this song."

From the speakers, Lizzo sang for the music to be turned up and the lights turned down. Mac rocked in her seat. Dani grinned and drummed her thumbs on the steering wheel. It was all she could manage. Then the song ended, and an advertisement asked whether they'd suffered a traffic accident and wanted to sue someone.

Mac sighed and flicked the advertisements off. She rolled down her window. Dani did the same.

The road unfolded in front of her. The color of the grass in the meadows rolled from a dusty brown to light green to a dark, verdant emerald in the dips where water collected. The trees ahead swayed in the breeze. It really took the edge off the day.

Dani checked the rearview and saw only an empty stretch of road behind them, identical to the empty stretch in front of them. She hoped they didn't blow a tire or hit a deer. Even AAA would have a hard time finding them out here. "I'm guessing that'll probably be the last interview I do for a while. I think I'll miss them. Even the ones with creepy guys."

Mac ran her fingers through her white-blond hair. The wind tried to tangle the short locks. "When are you going on maternity leave?"

"Next week, I think. Theo's been pushing me to do it for a while. I'd have probably done it last week if not for…you know."

"Right." Mac stretched her legs. The series of murdered cheerleaders had brought everyone out from behind their desks and into the field, even the cyber tech. "How long do you think you'll be out?"

"Don't know. I can take up to six months."

"Nice!"

"Without pay."

"Boo."

"Of course, if I come back earlier, a big chunk of the pay goes to daycare anyway. There's only so much babysitting we can drop on Theo's parents."

"Right." Mac fell silent.

Dani grinned. This was all a long way away for Mac. There were ten years between them, so Mac probably had a good decade before she had to start thinking about maternity leave. Six months with the baby was tempting, and Theo had just landed a promotion. Even with only one income for half a year, they should be able to manage.

But everything changed so fast at the FBI. She could come back in six months' time and find there was no one in the office she recognized.

Stella was new but already racing ahead, an indispensable member of the team. She could be promoted, leading the pack when Dani returned. Slade could move on or take early retirement. Chloe could transfer. Ander could move off to someplace closer to his son. Hagen had moved around a lot, but he seemed to have settled down in Nashville. Maybe he'd still be there in six months, smoldering away, ready to cut someone down with a sharp comment.

Six months. That feels like a lifetime.

Dani glanced at Mac, who was tapping on her phone.

Mac grinned. "Just texting Stella about the gym."

"Telling her about the creepy owner?"

"Yeah…and the view she'd get while working out."

"View? There were no windows there, and that place looked like it was a *men-only* joint."

Mac laughed.

What the hell?

She'd been so distracted by their conversation that Dani had stopped checking her mirrors every few minutes. From out of nowhere, an old beat-up truck was on their tail. She couldn't even read the license plate. Because it was that close.

She could see very little past the truck's windshield, except for a pair of meaty fists gripping the top of the steering wheel.

"What the hell?" she repeated, this time out loud.

"What?"

Dani nodded at the rearview. "Some jackass is on our ass."

Mac checked out the mirror on her side. "Whoa. Where did he come from?"

Dani pushed the gas. That lunatic was far too close.

The truck's engine roared in return. The truck drew closer, the cab filling the rearview mirror.

"What the hell is he doing?"

Mac turned in her seat. "Jesus. He's going to—"

The car jolted.

Dani clutched the steering wheel, her knuckles turning white. There was no place to turn off here. No shoulders. The road stretched on, the ditches on either side forcing her to drive straight. She put her foot down. The only way to avoid this guy was to pull way ahead.

If only she were driving Hagen's Corvette instead of this eco-friendly Civic.

The truck had fallen back, but it started gaining again. The driver's eyes were narrowed, his mouth curled into a savage snarl.

Mac tightened her seat belt. "What the hell is he trying to do?"

"He's trying to run us off the road. How far to the highway?"

Mac scrolled the satnav. "Er, a ways. About ten miles."

"Shit." Dani exhaled a long breath. "Call the sheriff's

office. They're closer. They might have a patrol out here." If they could reach the highway, they could escape this maniac. They had to get there.

Ten miles.

She put her foot down harder. The truck fell away.

The speedometer clicked up. Fifty miles an hour. Sixty. Too fast on a back road.

Mac's face was pale as she dialed. "I can't get a signal. Where the hell are we? I thought only Nebraska couldn't get cell service."

"You okay?"

Mac gave a hasty nod, trying again. "I'm fine."

Dani breathed out slowly. Her tactical driving courses were over a decade behind her, but she remembered to stay focused, to pay attention to the car. The Honda's engine whined. But the tires felt solid, handling the small bumps in the asphalt smoothly.

Again, the truck drew closer, the driver's hat pulled low over his eyes.

Dani swallowed.

This wasn't road rage. He wasn't using the horn or trying to get ahead.

"Hold on."

The car jolted again, and, this time, the front slid to the left. Dani pulled the wheel to the right. She eased up on the gas, then put her foot down slowly. The tires bit into the asphalt. The car righted itself.

"Dani." Mac pointed.

Directly ahead, the road curved. An old oak stood next to the bend, casting a welcome shadow over the meadow. A low branch stretched over the ditch. They were going too fast to make the corner. Dani lifted her foot off the gas. She touched the brake—

Thump. Crack.

Time slowed.

The weight that had grown steadily in Dani's belly over the last eight months shifted as the car skidded. As if from a distance, Dani noted they were spinning. The world was a blur of green and black roadway.

For a second, the cab of the truck pulled right next to them.

He was so close. She could almost reach out and punch the driver in the face.

But the truck dropped away as the front of the car rose and the back end slipped into the ditch. Dani jerked against the suddenly tight seat belt. Pain shot through her shoulder and along her lower abdomen. Her head banged against the headrest.

Mac made a strange, barking noise before growing quiet.

In slow motion, Dani's phone flew out of the cup holder and landed somewhere behind them.

In a month, there would be a baby's car seat back there where the phone had landed. Dani could imagine chubby little fingers and toes wiggling. A sudden burst of panic struck her hard in her chest as she wondered if she'd get to count those tiny digits.

Crunch.

The Honda's roof came down, making a wall between Dani and Mac. The windshield shattered into a frame of tiny, translucent jigsaw pieces as the branch of the oak tree wedged into the top of the car.

We hit the tree. Or the tree hit us.

The car shifted down again. Glass scratched across Dani's face and caught in her hair.

Then everything was still.

A coil of steam rose from the hood.

You're okay. You're good. Breathe.

Dani exhaled slowly.

"Mac?"

Silence.

Beneath the car's bent roof, Mac's arm hung limply. Dani's stomach twisted.

Off in the distance, a car door slammed.

The driver.

Anger burst through Dani. She pushed at the release for her seat belt.

Nothing happened. The button depressed, but the belt remained.

"Dammit. Come on!"

Again, she pushed the release button and tugged at the belt, which cut into her lower belly, making it difficult to breathe. Her phone was in the back, buried beneath bent metal. Everything was out of place.

Footsteps sounded heavy behind the car.

"Come on!"

She pulled again. The seat belt came free, and Dani reached for the door handle.

Please don't be jammed. Please just...

The door swung open.

Thank you, God.

She twisted in her seat and swung her legs out of the car. The grass was deep at the bottom of the ditch, and she landed with one leg resting against the bank. Once solid on the ground, she pulled her gun out of her holster.

The car's engine hissed like a bag of angry cats.

At the top of the ditch, the truck waited by the side of the road, its front fender bent, and its red paint marked by scratches and lines of rust.

There was no sign of the driver.

Dani licked her lips and held her weapon out in front of her, hating how badly her hands trembled.

Mac. Please be okay. I've got to get help.

She inched forward, making her way through the bottom of the ditch. The mud was wet under her feet, though it hadn't rained for days.

"Just put it down."

The voice came from behind her, deep and calm.

Her heart pounded, feeling like it might break free of her rib cage. Her palms were sweaty, and she wanted to wipe them on her trousers. Every muscle in her body vibrated.

She turned.

The driver crouched at the front of the car. It was the man from the gym, the one who'd watched them leave. Again, the small hairs on Dani's neck felt charged.

His tank top was stained with sweat, and his arms were outstretched, one hand supporting a gun in the other.

"I said *put it down*. Or I'll kill you and then I'll kill your friend. I won't say it a third time."

Dani wasn't going to put her gun down. She wasn't going to lose what little leverage she had. She was close enough not to miss—

Pain hit her, sharp and strong in her lower belly.

A contraction. Dani doubled over, an arm wrapped around her stomach. Still, she held her gun steady.

But he was quick. As she tried to breathe through the pain cutting across her abdomen, the man darted forward. She fired, but the shot went wide, hitting one of the tires.

He slammed into her.

She grunted as she began to fall. Dani tried to land on her side, protecting her baby. She'd never felt so exposed. Another contraction fired across her stomach.

No, baby, no. Not yet. It's not safe.

The man wrenched her wrist, and something popped an instant before pain exploded up her arm.

Though she did her best to grip the gun in her hand, her weapon dropped to the bottom of the ditch.

24

Stella shifted in her seat at the Nashville Resident Agency. Home base. Slade had wanted everyone in the office by three thirty. The meeting should have started ten minutes ago, but still, Mac and Dani weren't back.

Hagen sat opposite her, chatting with Ander about the length of pipe from the textile factory. Hagen was certain forensics would tell them that it had probably been used for moving heating oil through the old building.

Ander had his money on cast iron and believed it was part of the building's sprinkler system. He folded his arms and leaned back in the chair. "If I'm right, it could mean the perp's trying to send us a message. He knocks out a fire inspector using some fire safety gear. Coincidence?"

Hagen rolled his eyes. "What do you think the perp did with Carlos Guerrero? Hit him on the head with a traffic cone?"

Ander glared at Hagen, but there was no malice in it, just irritation.

Stella tried and almost succeeded at suppressing a smile. She turned to Chloe, who was busy tapping out a message one-handed on her phone. Chloe was the only person in the room who had someone waiting for them at home, someone wondering why they were sitting alone on a Saturday afternoon while their partner was back at work.

She touched the screen on her own phone, though she had no messages to send, and was relieved to find that her mother hadn't sent her one.

This job didn't make relationships easy to maintain.

But there was no message from Mac either. Or Dani.

Slade stuck his head in the doorway and took a quick head count. "They're still not here?"

No one spoke. Stella typed out a quick message to Mac.

Where are you guys? Slade is about to blow a fuse.

She sent it off…and waited. Then waited some more.

Stella swore quietly.

Slade took his normal spot in the front of the room. He leaned forward, pressing his hands into the table, seeming too angsty to sit. "Anyone heard from them?"

Stella held up her phone. "I texted Mac but no reply yet."

Slade tapped the table with his middle finger. "Keep trying. I suspect Dani's taken some country road without coverage and got stuck behind a tractor or something. Let me know as soon as you get anything. In the meantime, let's start. You can fill them in later."

Stella breathed out a long breath. Slade would probably go easy on them since he seemed more stressed at the team's absence than irritated. But once they were safely in front of him, that stress might morph into anger.

Chloe's phone beeped. Slade frowned at her. Chloe pushed her phone away and lifted her hand in apology.

Slade accepted with a small nod and then continued leading the briefing. "First things first, they've located Carlos Guerrero's cruiser. A gasoline can from the cruiser's emergency stash was found by the rear tires. Dented and with what could be blood on it. Guerrero's badge and gun were found on the driver's seat."

Hagen leaned forward. "Like Trang's badge and clipboard?"

"Looks like it."

Stella spun her gold stud. "So he's leaving the symbols and tools of their positions behind. Badges. Guns. Paperwork."

Slade nodded and pressed on. "We can connect the cases by the notes and now by what the perpetrator leaves behind. He appears to have some kind of grudge against authority." He looked around the room again.

Dani and Mac's absence grew heavier. Stella felt it.

"So I've just spoken to both Sheriff Marlowe and Ander's friend, Mick Ackhurst. Neither has had any contact with the missing deputy or the fire inspector. Hagen, you were looking into Victoria Trang. What have you got?"

Hagen ran a hand through his hair. Somehow, it fell perfectly back into place. "Not a lot. We spoke with her husband, Phil. He looks like he's in denial. Still working in his shop and expecting her to walk through the door at any moment."

"He give you any leads?"

"Not really. There've been a few racist attacks on his shop. We could look into those, but I think we'd do better to focus on companies his wife has fined. She did go missing at a company she'd just inspected."

Slade checked his watch again.

Stella felt the worry radiating off him. She checked her phone again. Nothing.

"Right. But we've got to draw a link between that company and Carlos Guerrero. And us. Stella, Chloe. You two find anything?"

Though she knew well enough what it contained, Stella pulled out her notebook. The move gave her a moment to collect her thoughts and shift them into some semblance of order. "We spoke to Carlos Guerrero's partner, Ezra Forman. He was pretty helpful."

"Well, I'd hope he would be."

Stella hesitated. The sarcasm was stronger than Slade usually threw. "Yeah. He mentioned an ex of Maria's who was a bit obsessed, a gym owner called Ivan Scheffler. We stopped by the house to speak to her about him. We got his contact information. Dani and Mac went to talk to him."

Slade pulled out his phone. "It would be a lot more useful if they were here to tell us what this Scheffler said. Where the hell are they?"

He lifted the phone to his ear. Almost immediately, he lowered it and tried again. When he lowered his phone for a second time, Stella's chest tightened.

"One of them should be available. If not Dani, then Mac. Both of them wouldn't have turned their phones off at the same time."

"It could be as simple as no service," Stella offered, but she could see from his slumped shoulders that he didn't think so.

Something has happened.

Silence settled over the room as heavy as a wet blanket.

Chloe pushed her seat back from the table. "We can find the last place their phones were active."

Everyone followed Chloe out of the conference room to her desk. The team gathered around her monitor. A dot appeared next to a small country road. "There they are."

Stella took a deep breath to calm her trembling nerves. "They lost service in the middle of nowhere more than an hour ago. That dead zone couldn't be that big."

Slade was already halfway out the office door. "Call the sheriff's office. Tell them we'll meet them at that GPS location. Let's go. Now."

25

Stella and Chloe reached the vehicle first, making Stella glad that the one-armed wonder had insisted on driving. The sight of the car took her breath away. She turned to Chloe, but Chloe nodded, not taking her eyes from the vehicle.

"I see it."

From a distance, the front of the silver car—bent and twisted and sticking up from the ditch—looked like an abandoned piece of scrap metal. An oak tree branch rested in a giant dent in the middle of the roof. It was only as they approached the bend in the road that she became certain the fender belonged to Mac's Honda.

Stella had the door open before Chloe was in park. She leapt into the grass and scrambled down the ditch. The car's roof was caved in. The windshield was shattered. The sides of the car were scraped and scratched. Mud and grass clung to the dents in the bodywork.

She shouted as she ran. "Mac! Dani!"

There was no reply.

Stella slid down the bank until she reached the driver's

door. The car was empty. On the driver's seat, a gun and a badge were neatly arranged. Just like Guerrero. And Trang. The message was clear.

Somehow, the person who had kidnapped one sheriff's deputy and one fire inspector had reached their team.

What are you afraid of, Paul Slade?

He'd disarmed them. He'd taken them.

For a moment, Stella stood frozen in a sea of fear and indecision. There was so little to go on. An empty car. Two missing friends. A missing baby.

Chloe reached the passenger side. She tugged at the door with her uninjured hand. The door creaked open by about a foot but wouldn't go any farther. No matter how hard she pulled, Chloe couldn't get leverage.

"There's no one there."

Chloe gave the door another hard yank. Then she screamed in frustration, cutting through the strange silence.

"Fuck this!" Chloe yanked at her shoulder sling. She pulled the shoulder strap over her head. Then she ripped open the section bracing her elbow. In one motion, she dropped the whole rig into the ditch. The sling landed in a puddle, splashing muddy water up onto Chloe's pant leg.

"Chloe, they're not—"

"I know. But look at the seat."

Stella scrambled around the car.

The Honda rocked in the ditch as Chloe yanked on the passenger door. She gained another six inches. She leaned in, aiming her flashlight at the seat. Another badge, another gun.

Stella dropped to her haunches and peered up under the caved-in roof. At the top of the passenger seat, from the bottom of the headrest and smeared down the back of the seat, was a long, dark stain.

Chloe followed the trail with her light. Two small drops

had landed on the edge of the seat, and three more had fallen into the passenger's footwell.

Stella fell back. Beside her, Chloe's discarded sling sunk into the wet grass of the ditch.

Pressure spread outward from her chest.

At least one of them was hurt. Either Mac or Dani. Or both.

Every possibility Stella contemplated competed with the next. Mac and Dani might, even now, be fighting their captor and winning. Or they could be wounded and unconscious. Or they might be dead and buried.

On the road, brakes screeched. A car door opened and slammed shut.

In seconds, Slade jumped into the ditch, landing with a quiet splash and the steady balance of a man ten years younger. He shoved past Stella and leaned into the car. His eyes were narrowed, his face set.

Almost immediately, he stepped back. His breathing came in slow, heavy movements as though he was trying not to explode, to calm his reaction.

Ander's car stopped behind Slade's SUV. In two steps, Slade was out of the ditch and striding toward Ander's door.

"They're not there. Turn this thing around. Get back to the junction and block all traffic. I'll call in a ten-mile perimeter and put out the BOLO. Make sure no one comes down here."

He spun around to Chloe. "You and Stella. Get after them. That bastard's got an hour on us, but he could still be in the area. I want him found. Now. Check every house, every barn, every hole." His eyes narrowed even more. "What the hell are you all waiting for? Go!"

The wheels of Ander's car spun on the asphalt. The car raced backward then darted forward, charging back to the junction of Montgomery Avenue.

Stella clambered up the side of the ditch, Chloe right behind her but moving fast. Stella yanked open the passenger door, strapped in, and barely got her leg inside before Chloe hit the gas. The acceleration forced the door closed, and the car leapt down the road, asphalt rattling against the chassis as Stella reached for the seat belt.

It was only as she pushed the clasp into place that she realized how heavily she was breathing.

Mac's gone. Dani's gone. One of them's hurt.

The baby.

Chloe's face was frozen. Both hands rested firmly on the steering wheel, as if being shot had never happened. Her eyes focused on the halfway point between the car and the line of poplar trees on the horizon. She knew.

An hour.

An hour was forever.

The pressure in Stella's chest solidified into a steel ball, solid and immovable as she scrolled the map on the satnav.

"There's a farmhouse about three miles up the road. Take the next right."

Chloe gave the smallest of nods. She put her foot on the gas.

Eighty miles an hour.

As the car sped down the road, Stella scanned the asphalt. She checked the meadows and tried to see past the trees and over the hedges. There was no sign that anyone had been there. No skid marks suggesting someone had tried to wrest control of the vehicle. This was just another quiet road in another quiet part of the state where nothing more exciting happened than the occasional sighting of a hawk taking out a rabbit.

One of them was hurt.

"There." Stella pointed to the dirt road that opened on the right.

"I see it." Chloe's voice was firm and sharp. Whatever she was holding in was on the edge of erupting, and Stella didn't want to be there when the explosion happened. Unless it happened when they caught the perp.

For that, she definitely wanted to be there.

Chloe yanked the steering wheel. The tires skidded, sending stones rattling onto the road behind them. The car bounced down the dirt lane.

After they traveled less than half a mile, the lane curved to reveal an old two-story house that must have been built before WWII. The wooden planks that made up the house's walls had long ago bleached in the sun, then darkened with age. The roof had a groove that probably sent rain where rain shouldn't go. A dip at the edge of the porch suggested not all the space at the front of the house was used, if any.

A barn stood on one side of the house. The large double doors were closed.

Chloe didn't decelerate. She maintained speed until the car was almost at the house before she slammed on the brakes. The tires skidded on the dirt. Stella slid forward in her seat, her belt engaging. Clouds of dust blurred around the windows. It took a moment before the world felt solid again.

Chloe released her seat belt. One hand traveled to the back of her gun.

"Easy, Chloe." Stella gripped the agent's arm, slowing her down. "We don't know they're here. They could be—"

Creak.

The door of the house swung open. A man stood in the doorway. He wore a plaid shirt and gray slacks that crumpled above his sandaled feet. His silver hair was tousled. The skin on his neck was loose above his collar. He must have been near eighty.

Behind him, a woman who couldn't have been much

younger wiped her hands on a dishcloth. Her apron was dotted with flour and her white hair was in loose curls. The top of her head barely reached her husband's shoulder.

Stella and Chloe climbed out of the car. Chloe still seemed twitchy, moving too quickly toward the porch. Stella rushed after her.

The man frowned. "Can I help you two?"

Stella stepped onto the porch, cutting across her partner. She pulled out her ID. "Special Agent Stella Knox with the FBI. This your home, sir?"

The man made a small grunt. "Has been for sixty years. And was my pappy's before that. You two ladies came all the way out here to hear the history of this ole thing…well, I got stories I can tell ya."

Chloe didn't laugh, didn't even smile. "Did a vehicle come this way? About an hour ago? Maybe less?"

The old man shrugged and shook his head. He turned to his wife. "You hear anything, honey? Your ears are in better shape than mine."

The old woman brushed some of the flour from her apron and tutted. "No one came this way. No one at all."

Chloe rocked on her heels. "You sure about that, ma'am?"

The woman fixed her gaze on Chloe. "Young lady, if a deer so much as leaves a dropping on that lane, I'd know about it. A car coming up here? That'd be…heck, that'd be the most exciting thing that's happened here in the last fifty years."

Stella offered a professional smile. "You mind if we take a look in the barn?"

The old man shrugged again. "Feel free. You can clear it up, too, if you want. Place has barely been used these last twenty years."

He stepped off the porch and led them to the barn. Easing the rusty chain off the handle, he pushed open one of the doors. A strong smell of bird droppings wafted outside. Straw coated the floor. An old tractor that should have been in a museum stood at one end. The place was empty. No footprints or tire tracks other than their own marred the surrounding area.

Stella nodded and extended her card. "Thanks. You hear anything strange, or you remember anything, you call us right away, okay?"

The man took the card and held it close to his nose. "Something strange, huh? Like two FBI agents turning up on my door ain't strange. Reckon that's the kind of strange happens about once every fifty years."

They returned to the car. As the satnav came back on, Stella scrolled the map. Half a dozen farms were scattered around the area. Sirens in the distance suggested the police were already building their perimeter. They'd reach those farms soon too. The road continued to a new housing development before linking up with the highway.

Stella fell back in her seat.

Her fellow agents, her friends, could be anywhere.

26

The FBI agent with the white-blond hair and the head wound had been easy. Slumped in the passenger seat, her head tilted to one side as blood dripped from her temple onto the car's upholstery.

The other one, the redhead, had more fight. That bitch had actually fired at me. Lucky for me, her body had betrayed her, giving me just enough time to rush her. Might have even broken her wrist before she hit the ground and curled around her stomach.

For a brief moment, I thought I'd overreached. *Knocking over a pregnant woman?*

I needed to be careful, though.

Injured animals were more dangerous. Pregnant or not, I needed to keep my eye on her.

She wasn't limber enough to dive after the weapon, though she tried.

It took a blow to the head with the butt of my Smith & Wesson to stop her. The hit didn't knock her out, but it dazed her enough that I managed to duct tape her hands and feet before tossing her into the extended cab seat. Who knew a pregnant woman could scuffle like that? For good measure, I tied her hands to the bar on the back of the passenger seat.

When I was satisfied that she was secure, I took her badge and laid it next to her gun in the driver's seat.

This mama bear might be worth her salt.

I pulled out the smaller one, her limp form almost weightless. Dropping her badge and weapon on the passenger seat, I almost wished I could be here to witness the other agents locate the clues.

I tucked her limp body onto the passenger side of my truck bench. Glancing into the back seat, I told the first agent exactly what I would do to her friend if she tried to be a hero. "Sit still. Behave. And maybe your girl here will live." My gun pressed into the blond agent's already-bleeding temple as we drove away.

"Sorry, Mac. But it's going to be okay. I'll get you out of here. I promise."

"Her name's Mac, huh? And what's your name, honey?"

"I'm not your honey. I'm FBI Special Agent Danielle Jameson, and you, my friend, are in a whole heap of trouble." The threat of her words was negated as she hunched over again. I didn't know a thing about baby birthing, but something was going on.

"You think I'm in a whole heap of trouble? Lady, I've got an FBI agent at the end of my Smith & Wesson. Looks to me like I've got a jackpot. You going to have that baby now?"

She rolled onto her side, almost out of view of the rearview mirror. With her hands secured, she could only curl up when the pain hit. "Don't worry. It's not labor. I think. Not yet anyway."

Agent Jameson exhaled slowly. "What you've got is a choice and a small amount of time to make it. Put that thing down now and hand yourself in. There's still a chance that you'll see daylight again in your lifetime. Keep going the way you are, though, and your next choice will be between the electric chair or lethal injection."

She didn't scare me. I was the one holding the gun, and she was the one with nothing but a baby on the way. "I've made harder choices than that."

I hit the gas. Every minute counted now. The FBI wouldn't take long to figure out something was wrong. The wheels spun. My heart pumped like a twelve-valve engine. What I'd done was un-freaking-believable. I'd saved the Feds 'til after the deputy and the fire inspector because I thought they'd be hard. They were the best trained, the most experienced, and the ones most likely to put up a fight.

I had figured, with a little difficulty, I'd be able to grab one agent, and my original plan involved the injured one. A woman. And now, here I was with two agents tied up in my truck.

"Two FBI agents in a single haul. Ain't nothing can stop me." I smacked the steering wheel.

I put my foot down until I reached the small copse of poplars that grew where the ditch rose to meet the road. I glanced in the mirror. Jameson lay on her side like she was fast asleep. Slowing, I turned into the woods.

There was a little dirt road leading to the property, not much more than a couple of long ruts in the grass running up the hill between the trees. I used to get out this way when I was a kid and my pa had grounded me. No one knew this way but me.

Wasn't long before I bounced up the lane to the rear of the barn. I pulled up under the tree shading the graves of the cop and the fire inspector.

I dragged the little one out first. She was still unconscious, but she had a pulse, and the bleeding had stopped. She was going to have a nasty headache when she woke up. I tossed her over my shoulder.

"Won't be too long now, honey. You'll wake up soon enough. And then you'll probably wish you hadn't."

"Let her go. She needs a doctor." Jameson took a deep breath and winced. "And so do I."

The last thing I'd anticipated was the presence of a baby. I actually had no idea what to do if she suddenly birthed a kid right in front of me. "You're having your baby now?"

"You'd like that, wouldn't you? No. Lying like this...it's not good for the baby and it's not good for me...I can't..." She wriggled, unable to quite turn over with her hands and feet bound.

"I'll be back in a minute for you. Just wait right there." I made a show of turning in a circle, admiring the forest all around me. "Oh, and if you want to scream, you go right ahead. Ain't no one round here for miles. All you'll do is disturb the crows and make your little one think her ma's some kind of crazy."

I left her there and carried the other agent into the barn. The tub was still in the corner, though I'd been tempted to move it in the middle of the room. Veronica had thrashed around quite a bit. She'd wet the straw and made the ground damp, but fresh air and a few hours had dried the puddle.

The crate leaned against the wall. I kicked it down so it was flat on the ground.

"Should've put the crate next to the tub, huh, Mac?" I patted the agent on her back. "The good inspector could have rinsed it out for you."

I dropped her into the crate. She landed with a *thump* and didn't move.

By the time I returned to the truck, Agent Jameson had managed to swing herself around. She sat on the edge of the truck's rear seat, her bound legs hanging. Her face was red, and there were tears in her eyes. She'd done a lot for someone in her condition.

"Get me out of here. Untie me, let me and Mac go. It'll go much better for you if you cooperate."

It was almost funny, her trying to talk her way out of this.

I pulled my knife out and cut the tape binding her ankles.

"Yes. That's a great start."

She was funny. "Oh, I'm not letting you go. You're just too heavy to carry in your condition." It was a lie. I could have carried her to the state line and back. Years of endurance and weight training.

"Then you're going to have to help me down. I can't jump like this. Please."

I hesitated. Jameson sounded too polite. Too reasonable. "Just don't try anything stupid, okay?"

She glared at me. "Try anything stupid? What do you think I'm going to do? Ask you to recommend a good preschool?"

I stood next to her with my gun aimed at her belly. She leaned on my shoulder and carefully lowered herself from the truck. As soon as she reached the ground, I took two paces back and waved my gun toward the barn.

"Where's Mac? What've you done with her?" She picked her steps carefully, making her gait slow. Her red hair was a tangle at her back. As she walked, her voice was surprisingly pleasant. "If you've hurt her, I swear to God, the things that'll happen to you. They'll make Abu Ghraib look like a damn holiday camp."

A cold wave washed over me as though she'd thrown a bucket of ice water.

Abu Ghraib prison. Iraq.

"What the hell would you know about that?"

She shot me a scornful glance. "Everyone knows what happened there. And if you've done anything to Mac, that's where you'll end up, friend. I'll find the deepest, darkest hole in the most forgotten corner of the planet and I'll make sure things happen to you that you can't even imagine."

I swallowed, believing she'd try. "Move. Go on."

She walked into the barn and stopped. A quiet thumping sound came from the crate. The other one must have woken.

"Mac!"

Agent Jameson waddled as quickly as she could across the barn, her hands still taped together. I let her go. I could shoot her from here, could shoot them both. But they needed to be tested first. Otherwise, what was the point?

When she reached the crate, she dropped to one knee and peered inside.

"Mac, are you okay?"

Mac's voice was weak and muffled through the walls of the box. "Yeah, I'm okay. Worst hangover ever. What…what's going on? Where am I? What…?"

"Enough." I kept the gun trained on the pair as I hauled over an old kitchen chair from the wall of the barn. It was covered in dust and decorated with patches of bird droppings.

But beggars can't be choosers.

"Sit."

Agent Jameson pushed to her feet, surprisingly graceful with a round belly and no arm movement to balance her. "Everything's going to be okay, Mac. They're looking for us, and when they find us, they're going to do things to this guy that would make Freddy Krueger blanch."

"Who?" Mac's voice echoed inside the crate. "Who's there?"

I waved the gun again.

Jameson sat with a loud groan. Despite the dirt on the seat, she even sighed as she leaned back. Her relief eased some of my tension.

I didn't want to hurt a pregnant woman. That wasn't what I'd planned at all.

But I wanted someone strong. Trained. Powerful. Courageous. Jameson fit the bill nicely, which was a pleasant surprise.

And it was obvious what made this pregnant woman frightened. She was scared something might happen to her baby. A mother *should* be scared of losing her kid. That's not a fear they should ever lose.

Not that my ma ever cared what happened to me.

The mission. Complete the mission.

I pulled the duct tape roll out of the pocket of my sweats, holstered my weapon, and strode to the chair. Crouching, I pulled the length of tape around the back of the chair leg.

Jameson twisted, moving so fast I almost didn't see her in my peripheral vision. A blinding smack of pain burned through the side of my head as her foot smashed into my temple. I fell on my side, landing in the dust and straw.

My fingers dropped into the remains of a squashed tarantula.

She was out of that chair far faster than I could anticipate. Her foot drew back and swung toward my cheek.

I rolled. Her foot connected with the back of my head, a scuffed kick that knocked my chin to my chest. Her friend shouted from the box. "Dani! What's going on?"

She didn't take the time to answer and kicked again. This time, I caught her ankle and pulled.

Her center of gravity was off, and she hit the ground. Hard. Somehow, she pivoted to avoid landing on her belly. I found myself admiring her athletic ability, even though she was working at such a disadvantage.

I scrambled to my feet, yanking out my gun and pointing it at her. The weapon shook in my hand, pissing me off. I blinked to soothe my burning eyes.

"Get back in the chair. Now! Go on." Without waiting for her to climb up, I gathered a handful of her bright red hair and yanked. Jameson scrambled, trying to get her feet under her.

I practically threw her into the chair. The whole situation made me feel like a caveman. I didn't like the sensation.

My breath came in short pants. I worked my jaw and rubbed the side of my head where her kick had landed. She was dangerous, that one.

But so was I.

In one swift motion, I turned the gun in my hand and lunged. A satisfying *crack* of the gun striking her temple filled the air. She barely managed to keep herself upright.

"Dani?!"

Ignoring her partner, I bent down to tape her ankles to the chair legs. Removing the tape from her wrists, I yanked her arms behind her back before wrapping them again.

"Hitting a pregnant woman? Real tough." Her voice was weaker than before, but she'd recover quick. She'd be more dangerous in a minute.

"I'm a feminist. Equal treatment." I pressed the steel muzzle into her belly. She flinched. "Now, one more word, one more *blink*, and I'll shoot that kid right through your gut."

That did the trick.

Keeping my weapon trained on the chair, I walked to the crate, never turning my back on Jameson. She was stunned but not helpless.

Mac was lying there, just as the other two had done. She was smaller than the others, so she had more wiggle room, but not much. Her arms were bound behind her, which seemed just as uncomfortable for her as the previous two occupants. She wriggled from one side to the other and then up and down. It was a strange sight. Then I realized she was measuring the box. Figuring out its parameters.

A warmth grew within me, a great ball of hot confidence that spread from my guts to my limbs. She could wiggle all she wanted. She wasn't getting out. I'd built the crate to take more punishment than that slip of a girl could ever give.

I'd taken on the police and the fire department already. I was braver than both of them.

Now, I would prove I was braver and smarter than the FBI too. I leaned over the crate, whispering through the gaps between the wood planks.

"Mac, is it? Is that your name?"

"Yeah. Who the hell are you?"

"I'm the one asking the questions. And I've got a doozy for you. What are you afraid of, Mac?"

27

Stella squatted to stretch out her lower back. There were limited seating options in the on-site HQ tent they'd set up near the accident site. Her hands were between her knees, holding onto a phone that didn't ring. Just yesterday morning, she'd been at the Resident Agency, holding a yellow piece of paper that seemed like a prank.

What are you afraid of, Paul Slade?

The "case" had seemed silly, a chance to get out of the office. To dodge and further delay some paperwork. A note. A deputy on a bender. The fire inspector was barely on anyone's radar.

Within thirty-six hours, Mac and Dani were missing. And this afternoon, Stella was afraid. Four hours had passed since they'd found the car and, still, no sign of the two women.

She and Chloe had driven from one farmhouse to another, knocked on doors, and peered through the windows of abandoned buildings. This rural area seemed pockmarked with small outbuildings. It would take forever to identify owners and go through the properties. They had found no sign, no clue, no indication—other than the crashed car—that Dani and Mac had been in the area.

Anger, fear, and frustration gnawed at her. Each emotion brought its own set of sharp teeth to scrape and bite at her insides. She wanted to kick the walls down. As she stood up, her back and knees popped, providing a moment of relief.

Slade met her eye from across the folding table. Even in a small tent, with radios squawking and stone-faced deputies striding in and out of the entrance, Slade seemed in control. His direct gaze told deputies and agents to give clear and accurate reports. Wasting his time was unacceptable. He raised his eyebrows, looking for an update.

Stella shook her head. The deputy waiting in Maria Guerrero's house had nothing to report. The Trang team was equally silent. There was no contact from either Dani or Mac. The longer they went without news, the worse the situation became.

Slade's phone rang. He waved away a deputy who, to Stella's eye, seemed to be sitting around. Slade lifted the phone to his ear. "Go ahead."

He listened to the report, then turned to face the back wall of the tent, which had been converted into a large screen. A portable projector turned the white canvas into a map. Straight lines divided the meadows and woods into neat, colored sections.

Slade had given Stella and the team Zone C. They hadn't found so much as a crumb so far.

There was one K-9 unit. Drones were being deployed, but heavy tree cover made air search difficult. Slade called in more search teams from the FBI, but they took a while to arrive on the scene. Word had also gotten out to the press, who were bombarding the sheriff's office and the Resident Agency.

As Slade listened to whoever was on the other end of the

line, he highlighted a cluster of houses between Montgomery Avenue and the river and blacked out that section of the grid.

Stella sighed. More nothing.

Over two thirds of the map remained lit. A deputy strode into the tent, slid a note onto the table, and walked out without acknowledgment. Slade hung up, propped his reading glasses on his nose, and read the note. He leaned over his laptop again. A set of squares at the western end of the map turned dark.

"More K-9s have arrived."

Outside the temporary setup, police were leading dogs through fields, going door to door through housing projects, and scouring farms and old agricultural buildings. They shone flashlights into basements and dissected screens of telephone data, looking for a pattern that might reveal where Dani and Mac could be. Cops and agents from surrounding counties had been mobilized. Stella had never seen such a large effort pulled together in such a brief span of time.

She hoped she never would again.

She focused on the map for the thousandth time. There was still so much left to search, so many places where the kidnapper could have taken Dani and Mac. Miles and miles of fields and woods and homes and creeks and…

"Dammit."

Stella kicked a stray rock out the entrance. Distantly, she heard an "ow."

Slade lowered his reading glasses. "Get some air, Stella. You'll be heading back out soon. I need you fresh and alert. We could be in for a long night. I'll send the next search coordinates to Ander."

Stella took a deep breath and calmed herself. She left the tent.

Outside, it was bright from floodlights, and the field was crawling with people. Well, mostly their shadows, shuffling about like ghosts in a graveyard. Without paying much attention, she grabbed a Styrofoam cup of coffee, disappointed there was no hot chocolate. There was nothing sweet out here. Only bitterness.

Two deputies moved past her, heading into Slade's makeshift control room.

Hagen sat on a tree root. Between his fingers, he held a coffee cup identical to Stella's. It was the third coffee Stella had seen him drink since the team had come to the temporary HQ for a break, to catch up with Slade, and to receive a new set of grid squares to search. How he avoided being as jumpy as a rabbit on a trampoline, she had no idea.

She sat next to him, cradling her coffee, and stretched her legs. The first sip burned her tongue, but that was okay because it dampened the tar-like flavor.

Chloe leaned against the trunk of another tree. Both of her arms were free. One hand held an empty coffee cup, which she was using as an ashtray. Her other hand held a cigarette. The tip glowed in the dark. Stella had never seen her smoke before.

Without making eye contact, Chloe held the death stick out to Stella, offering a drag.

For a moment, Stella was tempted. "I'm not there yet."

Somewhere above them, a helicopter made a loud *thwop-thwop*. A beam of white light sliced a cone through the early night's darkness. The bottom of the cone landed in fields somewhere to the east.

Hagen fidgeted with his now-empty cup. "Anything?"

Stella shook her head. "Nothing. Not a sign."

"Mm." Hagen folded the edge of the cup inward and sighed. "I know you and Mac have gotten pretty close since you arrived. She's stronger than she looks, you know. Dani too. Whoever took those two is in for a rough ride."

Stella tried to smile. Hagen was trying to help, but he wasn't making much progress.

Dani was hardly at her fittest, and Mac...Mac belonged behind a keyboard, not in the field, and certainly not in the hands of some crazy kidnapper. Sure, she was stronger than she looked, but that didn't mean she was strong enough.

Oh, Mac. Please be okay. Please. I need you.

Stella took another burning sip of coffee. Maybe the heat could numb her.

This is what happens when you let someone in. You build bonds, deepen empathy. Care. Eventually, another someone comes along and tears it all away.

Every time.

Though her thoughts were on point, Stella felt selfish for having them. This wasn't about her. She shoved them back into a dark corner of her mind.

Chloe drew on her cigarette. The tip glowed angrily. "How's Slade doing?"

Stella shrugged. "Hard to say. Man's halfway to a robot right now. He's so focused on getting the search done. But I'm sure he's as cut up as the rest of us under there. He ever lost anyone under his command before?"

"No." Chloe jammed the end of the cigarette into the tree trunk. Embers erupted from the bark and rained to the ground. "And now he could lose two in one night."

No one spoke. The tent flap opened. Ander came out, his face drawn, his phone in his hand.

"Got new search coordinates. There's a bunch of farmhouses on it. Let's go keep some people awake."

28

I took a slug of my beer and kicked at the dry ground outside the barn. Dust floated up.

The whole situation was frustrating as hell.

That was the problem with opportunity. Fortune had dropped two agents right into my lap. I would have been some kind of fool to let that chance pass. But I hadn't been able to do any research. I didn't know anything about them.

The other ones had been easier.

I'd heard all about Veronica Trang and her bitchy inspections before I took her. Ivan from the gym had no problem sharing his frustration. I'm a very good listener. Then I'd heard about her next victim because it was another one of my friends. A military man no less.

When she came into his business for an inspection, I was ready. I followed her out. I was able to learn. I listened. I overheard. When cafés are small and voices are loud, you can pick up a whole heap of useful information. And where to find more. She even talked about when she was going to write her report, how much she'd fine him, and when she was returning with the ticket. So proud of herself.

The cop was even easier. A cop, sworn to uphold truth and justice, stealing another man's woman. He seemed perfect. Follow the threads and you can piece together all kinds of intel.

These two agents, though…this was a whole different ball game.

The pregnant one was obvious. I didn't even need to ask. It was easy as hell to put the fear of God into her. Her weakness was there for everyone to see, poking her shirt out.

I walked away from the barn and leaned against the big, old maple tree, weary to the bone. I closed my eyes and had trouble opening them again.

When had I last slept? Two nights ago? Three?

It didn't matter. I had a mission to complete.

Shaking my head to rid it of the spiderwebs wanting to take over, I pressed a hand to my stomach as nausea threatened to sneak up on me. And when had I last eaten?

Again…it didn't matter.

Nothing would get in the way of what I needed to do.

Can I really do this?

My stomach roiled again, but this time it wasn't from hunger. The thought of frightening a pregnant woman made me queasy, though I'd never show it.

No weakness.

To threaten her baby, I'd have to do more than pistol-whip her. I'd have to pull out my knife, make her believe I was going to cut that thing right out of her body. My very own do-it-yourself cesarean section.

Taping her to the chair had been hard enough, but I could relax a little after that. Though covering her mouth helped my blood pressure out a little more. There's only so much cussing a man wants to hear, especially when it's aimed right at him.

Still, actually killing a baby and a mother? With a knife? Maybe it was a step too far.

I took another sip of beer, looking for some courage, and let the bottle dangle from my fingers.

No one does a thing like that.

When my eyes threatened to close again, I pushed myself away from the tree and paced back toward the house, shaking more spiderwebs from my brain.

Heck, what are you talking about? Plenty of people do.

I'd seen the videos, the ones that got blocked on YouTube but were shared around on Telegram and other places, like a secret bottle of hooch on a dry base. I knew what happened in war zones, in the heat of battle. I'd seen it. Soldiers knew how to numb their feelings and did what they had to do.

Complete the mission. That was all that mattered. Make sure these people were worth their badges.

That's what I was going to do. That's what I was always going to do. Nothing would stop me.

I chugged down the last of the beer and let the bottle drop to my hip. It felt good in my hands. There's so much damage you can do with a glass bottle. A slash with some sharp broken glass would tear through a tight-skinned belly. As good a weapon as any, a beer bottle, and always available. Right there when you needed it.

"Yeah, one way or another, I'll get the mission done."

But I'd try with the other one again first, save the knife work for later.

Right now, I needed to know what Mac was scared of. I already knew her partner's greatest fear.

Just a shame she'd been so uncooperative until now. I didn't know what they taught them in the FBI about holding up under interrogation, but it must be good. So far, she hadn't given away a damn thing.

Mac did have a thorough and strong command of curse

words. A small thing like that should have been ashamed of herself. She had words I hadn't learned until I went into basic training.

But her fears eluded me. She didn't flinch when I held a lighter close to her fingertips until the fire went out. She actually giggled when I dropped one of the leftover spiders down her collar. The spider was still in her shirt. Nothing moved her at all. These attempts bothered Jameson more than they did Blondie.

Gotta admit, I was kinda impressed. Even thought I might have found someone genuinely worthy. Maybe I should let her go.

I could just see myself dragging her out of the crate, cutting the tape around her ankles and wrists, and throwing open the barn door.

"Go on." That's what I'd say. *"You deserve it. Be on your way now, brave girl, and thank you for your service. You can even take your friend with you."*

I chuckled, my laughter disappearing over the fields.

Like that was ever going to happen.

Naw, everyone had their breaking point. I just needed to find hers. I'd been patient so far.

It was time to raise the stakes a little.

I hurled the empty bottle toward the trees. It dropped into the undergrowth with a quiet *thud*. I cracked my knuckles and headed back toward the barn. This was going to be good.

A low rumble from somewhere behind stopped me. Headlights moved up the lane from the road.

A car. The police. It had to be. Or someone else looking for my detainees.

I froze. I just couldn't move. The lights grew closer, flickering between the tree branches. Suddenly, the world seemed filled with shifting shadows, men with guns creeping closer.

The engine rumbled and growled. Like Iraq. I stayed in place, my feet rooted to the ground. I told myself I was waiting for them to pass by.

"In here. We're in here!"

One of the agents had heard the car, the little one.

Shit. I didn't gag her after the spider.

I had to move. The barn walls weren't thick. Sound traveled in areas this desolate.

Her call for help unfroze me. I ran around the barn to the side door and pulled it closed behind me. The place only had one light, a bare bulb hanging from the ceiling and casting little more than a dull glow over the big, empty space inside. I turned it off and lowered the latch on both doors.

The rumble of the car drew closer. It sounded like a tank.

"We're in here!"

I ran to the crate and aimed my gun at her. "Not another word. I'll kill you both."

She fell silent, as I expected she would. There weren't many people brave enough to resist a gun pointed at their face. I leaned closer.

The pregnant one, Agent Jameson, shuffled in her chair. *"Hnn. Hnnnn."*

I didn't have to worry about her. She wasn't going anywhere, and she couldn't say anything louder than a grunt. Quietly, I crept to the wall of the barn. Through the slats, I watched the car pull up outside the farmhouse.

It wasn't a police car. Must have been some other agency, maybe even the FBI. The doors opened, and two people got out. I could barely see them in the darkness, but that just made them even scarier. My mouth was dry as dust, and my heart raced like a dragster.

"Hnn."

I spun around. "Shh!" I whispered but struggled to keep my voice down. "Or one of you dies right now."

The barn fell silent again. I turned back to the crack in the wall. A figure stood on the farmhouse porch. Someone else waited behind them.

Please go away. Please, please, just go away!

My gun trembled in my hand.

Thump. Thump.

A bang on the door. My breath came heavily. My legs turned to wet spaghetti. I had to lean against the wall to hold myself up.

Nothing there, Officer. And you've got no just cause, so get lost. Go on, now. Please!

I wasn't afraid. Not exactly. I'd gone on this mission knowing I could be caught or killed. What frightened me most was the idea that I might die before finding someone deserving of my leniency.

One of the figures moved away from the door. A beam of light shot from shoulder height at the window of the farmhouse.

The nerve of those guys, shining their light into my home.

Drifting away, the beam lit up the fields, passed over the narrow lane, and landed on the big maple tree. Its low branches hid much of the barn. It stayed there for a moment, the white circle turning the bark of the tree into deep ravines and the branches into grasping arms.

The light went off. Two doors slammed, and the rumble of the car receded into the distance.

"Hnn. Hn, hn."

Agent Jameson's grunts had turned into cries of frustration. I grinned and tucked my gun back into its holster. A towel hung from a hook on one of the beams. I pulled it down and slapped it over my shoulder.

Time for little Mac to *show* me what she was afraid of.

29

Stella peered through the windshield. There were no lights on these country roads, and it was hard to make out anything beyond the glow of the car's headlights. But there was a pair of headlights shining their white LED glare into the surrounding fields.

Chloe steered the vehicle to the shoulder. "There's Ander and Hagen."

"What makes you so sure it's them?"

Chloe pulled up behind the dark car. "Who else would be out here in the middle of nowhere this time of night? We're the only ones in this zone."

"Bad guys, maybe." Stella eased off her seat belt as the car slowed to a halt.

A blast of cicadas and distant frogs greeted her. They were definitely not in the city. The night sky overhead blazed with stars, which just made the landscape appear that much darker.

Chloe was right. Ander sat in the driver's seat of the other car, and Hagen leaned against the side, one hand jammed into the small of his back. A copy of the giant map in Slade's tent showed on the laptop mounted between the driver and passenger seats. More black squares marked searched areas. Infrared drone footage showed treetop after endless treetop.

"Take it you didn't find anything?"

Hagen dropped his arm, hiding the smallest of sweat stains appearing on his polo shirt. The stress and heat were having an impact on the clean-cut agent. "No. Ander's calling in a whole lot of nothing right now."

"Guess we should add our pile of nothing to it." Stella tapped on Ander's window. He lowered the glass.

"Just a second, boss. Here's Stella."

Slade's voice rasped through the car's stereo system. "Stella, what have you got?"

Stella hesitated. She hated reports like these. "Nothing. We'll take another sweep in the morning, though. Can't see a damn thing out here."

"Right." Slade's voice was sharp, curt. "I've got another farm for you. I'll send the coordinates to Ander." A crackle of static sounded as Slade disconnected.

Chloe reached the car as Ander's phone pinged. "What did we score this time?"

Ander checked the screen. "Let's see. Oh, it's not Slade. Mick Ackhurst, the fire chief. I was talking to him earlier."

Hagen met them at Ander's open door. He arched his back, releasing a loud crack. Stella almost laughed. He was falling apart tonight. "They hear anything from Veronica Trang?"

"No. But he sent me a list of all the places Veronica Trang inspected over the last six months. He says he can go back earlier if we need to."

Stella knelt next to Ander, her heels digging into the soft earth. She reached over and tilted Ander's phone toward her. "Let me see." He let her, but he didn't let go of his phone, so she cradled his hand in hers. "If we cross-check the owners of those businesses with properties in this area, we might be able to narrow the search."

Ander scrolled the screen. "That could take a while, even if we only focus on the places she's fined."

The document rolled up the page. Restaurants, factories, office buildings, and apartment blocks followed one after the other.

Hagen peered over Stella's shoulder. For a moment, his breath, smelling of stale coffee, brushed her cheek. Then he stood. He slammed his palm against the roof of the car. "Christ, that'll take forever."

Stella narrowed her eyes, letting go of Ander's hand. She spoke quietly. "Stop."

Ander continued scrolling, his thumb dragging the page and revealing yet more names of businesses with fire certificates to maintain. A familiar name flashed across the screen.

"Wait." Stella put her hand over the back of his. "Stop. Go back."

Without pulling his hand away, he scrolled the page down.

Stella took a sharp breath. Excitement kicked away the fear and anger that had been chewing on her guts for the past six hours.

Ivan's Gym.

"That's the last place Dani and Mac were. Right before their accident."

Chloe flicked her cigarette onto the road. "Yeah. He's Maria's ex."

Stella lifted Ander's phone. "Trang inspected the gym."

"You're telling me this guy has connections to all the victims at this point?" Hagen sounded dangerously calm now. "Guerrero, Trang. And our people were last seen in his vicinity?"

In the light of the stars, Chloe's smile was bright and feral.

"That's what we're telling you." Her anxious energy showed she was ready for action after sitting things out for so long. She headed to the car.

Stella gripped Ander's shoulder. "Tell Slade to hold off on that farm. We need to go back to that gym."

30

Hagen felt the vibration of the techno-beat workout music in his sore backside. Only a handful of spaces were left in the parking lot behind Ivan's Gym. The rest of the lot was filled with pickups, ramped-up SUVs, and a couple of low-slung Camaros. The place seemed hopping for almost ten p.m.

He stepped out of the car and waited for Ander to join him, unsure if they were about to walk into a gym or a weird workout-based nightclub. "If I'd known the place was going to look like this, I'd have shaved your hair down the sides. A curly mullet would help you fit right in."

Ander closed the door and locked it. He eyed Hagen's polo shirt, his pressed slacks, and brown Italian Oxfords. "Not if I came with you, it wouldn't."

Stella and Chloe pulled into the space next to them.

Hagen headed to the entrance. They would catch up.

Opening the door, the sound turned into a loud *boom-boom-boom* that thrummed through the soles of Hagen's feet.

"Jesus, what is this crap?" he whispered, though he

doubted that Ander, standing right behind him, would have heard even if he'd shouted.

The place was packed. Lines of men—and only men—in tank tops and taped fists punched swinging leather bags. Other men lifted overloaded barbells that bowed in the middle. Their grunts were louder than the music. A weight clanged back into place that was quickly followed up with, "That's what I'm talking about!"

Hagen strode up the middle of the gym. Hard looks sized him up. For a brief moment, a sense of inadequacy rolled over him. Outside the gym, he was muscular but lean. Inside, surrounded by bodybuilders, he looked like the *before* picture in an old Charles Atlas bodybuilding ad.

The feeling passed quickly. Hagen's deltoids might not have been the size of half a watermelon, and his biceps could fit through the sleeves of a regular t-shirt without tearing them, but at least he wasn't overcompensating for anything.

He'd seen men like these too often. They worked as bouncers outside nightclubs or, if they were lucky, some dealer or gang leader would tip them extra and employ them as enforcers. Their appearance alone would be enough to shake money out of a frightened debtor or calm an angry, cheated customer. His father had defended several guys like that in his career.

Their big, bad, muscular fronts would collapse pretty quick when they were arrested. On more than one occasion, he'd walked into his dad's office to see a giant bruiser breeze past him dabbing his sleeve to his eyes still red with tears. They might have been physically strong, but at the slightest psychological pressure, men like these deflated faster than burst balloons.

And it was hard to respect guys who didn't have anything better to do on a Saturday night.

As the door opened again behind him, the atmosphere in

the room changed. When the men had seen Hagen and Ander, there had been a few silent nods of acknowledgment before a fist smacked into a punching bag again or a weight was yanked into the air.

But with the arrival of Stella and Chloe, everyone froze. In the corner, a man with a blond flattop and a face redder than a stop sign froze mid-spot to glare at the new arrivals.

Crash.

A shirtless youth with only the barest of baby muscles fell from a pull-up bar and landed in a heap on the floor. He picked himself up and brushed the dust from his shorts, grinning sheepishly.

Hagen wanted to laugh but instead focused closer on the men's behavior. They all seemed to take in the women's presence and not all with harmless curiosity.

Chloe's black t-shirt and black jeans, her cropped black hair, and the scowl that seemed to have settled permanently onto her face since they'd found the car that afternoon demanded respect. But she was antagonistic, and her set jaw was a mirror to these unsmiling men.

Stella always drew attention because of her obvious attractiveness and the confidence she exuded. That combination of beauty and bearing was catnip to men like these. Certainly, in some of their eyes, there was a hard focus. On others, leering grins that put Hagen on edge.

The door to the office at the end of a hallway opened. The man who emerged should have been working in a barber shop. His thick beard, the gel in his black hair, and the closely shaved sides of his head all suggested he was someone who spent far too much time in front of a mirror.

He gripped a towel tightly in his fist. As he strode through the gym to meet them, the men left their punching bags and their weights and drew closer, as if the gym were a playground and a fight was about to ensue. Soon, only a handful of the men were still sprawled on benches or sitting by lockers. The rest formed a loose circle around Hagen, Ander, Stella, and Chloe.

Hagen pulled out his ID. "Ivan Scheffler? We're with the—"

Ivan slapped the towel over his shoulder as he entered the circle of men. "You're with the FBI. Yeah, yeah, I know. Had a couple of you in here earlier. Now they send four of you, huh? And all this just to hear about my ex. Gotta tell you guys, she really wasn't that special."

Ivan was a tall man. He stood with his broad shoulders thrown back and his hands on his narrow hips. Hagen stared him straight in the eye.

"The two agents who came here. What time did they leave?"

Ivan shrugged. He turned to the man sitting in the corner by the lockers. He wore a tank top just like Ivan's with the word COACH across the front. "Bill, you were here then. What time did those two women leave today?"

Bill shrugged and scratched his shaven head. "Which women is that?"

Hagen rolled his eyes. He doubted anyone in this gym had seen more than three women in their life and none, other than Mac and Dani, between these walls. He didn't have time for this crap. "You know which women. I'll ask one more time and then I'm going to get annoyed. What time did they leave?"

Bill leaned back on the bench. "I wasn't wearing a watch, but if I had to guess...well, I'd say they arrived around midday, and they weren't here too long. Maybe around twenty minutes or so, less probably. Wouldn't you say that, Coach?"

Ivan nodded. "Yeah. Yeah, I'd say that, Coach." He looked

at the circle of men surrounding Hagen and the others. "You guys all agree?"

The men nodded, though Hagen doubted that any of them had been here then. Ivan Scheffler could get these guys to say anything.

Ander stepped forward. "Got any security footage so we can pinpoint a time?"

Ivan sized Ander up. Then he turned to one of the men wearing a blue t-shirt labeled PERSONAL TRAINER. "Joey, you want to take this one and look at security footage of this afternoon?" Joey nodded, then walked away, clearly expecting Ander to follow.

"Chloe, come with me." The pair followed Joey the Personal Trainer to a cluster of television screens in the corner of the gym near another row of lockers. Hagen couldn't hear their discussion over the throbbing music.

Stella addressed Ivan. "They asked you about Maria?"

Ivan snorted. "Yeah. Waste of time. Told them I haven't spoken to Maria since she married. Whatever she's done has nothing to do with me."

"Let's talk over here." Stella led the way to a spot near the other set of lockers, farther away from the men who were still lingering.

They walked past the gym equipment, just the three of them now. Hagen leaned against the corner of the lockers and folded his arms over his chest. A few feet away, it seemed like Ander was asking Joey the Personal Trainer to rewind some footage. Hagen kept them in his peripheral vision as he spoke to Ivan.

"Veronica Trang. Remember her?"

Ivan shook his head. "Never heard of her."

Stella took out her phone and consulted the fire inspection document Ander had shared with her. "She fined you two hundred and fifty bucks for fire code violations about four weeks ago."

Ivan took a deep breath. He rubbed his beard, sending small flakes of dead skin to float gently to the gym mat. "Oh, her. Yeah, she was a real pain in the ass."

"You tell her that?"

"Told her a lot of things. None of which I care to repeat to you."

A sharp movement caught Hagen's eye. Ander was pointing to a screen with a bit too much enthusiasm.

He found something.

Hagen rested more of his weight against the locker bay. "And why's that?"

"Because I'm a gentleman." Ivan waved his hand at Stella, both acknowledging and dismissing her at the same time. "And I don't want to use that kind of language in front of a lady."

Stella laughed, but there was no humor in it. "But you used that language in front of Veronica Trang."

"Woman who comes in here and tries to tell me what to do with my business is no lady."

"When was the last time you saw her?"

Ivan shrugged. "When she did the fire inspection, I guess. We don't hang out."

Whatever Ander saw, Hagen hoped it was good because he was losing patience with Ivan Scheffler.

Mac and Dani were in danger, and they were getting the runaround from a muscle head.

He spoke calmly but deliberately. "I want you to listen to me, Ivan, and I want you to listen very carefully. We've got a missing deputy who's married to your ex-girlfriend. We've got a missing fire inspector who fined your business. And now we've got two FBI agents who were last seen in this very gym not more than a few hours ago. You're the only thing that connects all these missing people, which means that, right now, you're likely heading to a very small cell with a very long sentence."

Ivan swung the towel back over his shoulder. "Nothing to do with me. And if you'll excuse me, it's late, and I've got stuff I need to do." He turned and headed past the lockers for his office.

A fire burst in Hagen's chest. The flame had been building all afternoon, growing on a diet of worry and frustration and anger, on negative reports from the searchers, and on the images in his head of Dani and Mac.

Ivan was a big guy, but he wasn't too big to hit the ground hard.

Hagen took half a step—

Ander reached them before Hagen could do what he *really* wanted to do—put a foot up Ivan's ass.

"Hold up, Mr. Scheffler." Ander beelined to the wall of lockers and shimmied his arm behind them. He pulled out a large freezer bag stuffed with small, white pills. "Mr. Scheffler, it seems you've been allowing drug usage on the premises. Perhaps even using yourself?"

Hagen smiled. "Now, isn't that sweet?"

In one move, Hagen had Ivan on the ground, his hands pinned behind his back. Ivan's beard was embedded in the gym's floor mat.

Chloe stepped in front of two men who wanted to get into the mix.

"Anyone interferes and you'll get the same." The men stepped back with their hands raised.

Hagen glanced up at Stella. "You want to cuff him? Let's call it in and get him back to the station. He's gonna spill."

31

Ander and Chloe held open the doors to the Pelham Sheriff's Office as Stella and Hagen pushed Ivan Scheffler inside.

The place fell silent. Officers looked up from computer screens and lowered their phones. Keyboards stopped clicking. A conversation by the vending machine about a cluster of houses that still needed to be searched came to an end mid-sentence.

Ezra Forman, Carlos's partner, pushed out of his chair. He took the bag of pills from Ander, turning them over in his hand, and grasped Ivan's upper arm. His fingers bit deeply into the man's skin, but the gym owner didn't wince.

Stella released her grip. "Get him booked in."

As Ezra took him away for fingerprinting and booking, Slade rushed in the main doors behind them. His slacks and shoes were dirty from the field site, and he left a small trail of dirt on the entrance mats. "Good work. You think he took them?"

Hagen gave a short nod. "Wouldn't bet my house on it, but yeah. Can't be a coincidence that he's connected to everyone who's gone missing. He gets rid of Carlos, maybe he thinks he can get his ex back. Veronica Trang hurt him so he's hurting her back. It clicks."

"Stella?"

Stella turned her ear stud. She hesitated before answering. "I'm not sure. If he wanted Maria back, he's moving late. Not many men want to raise some other man's kid. Veronica Trang fined him, but not much, and that was a few weeks ago. Abducting her seems like a hell of an overreaction. And what did Mac and Dani do other than ask him a few questions about Maria? I dunno. That said, there's a connection here. I'm just not sure what it is."

Slade rocked on his heels. "Chloe? Ander?"

Chloe glanced at Stella. "I'm with her. Can't be a coincidence that he's connected to all three of them, but someone who'd abduct a cop and three women? I'm not sure he's got that in him."

Ander shrugged. "I do. The bigger the ego, the thinner the skin. Man who spends that much time in front of a mirror flexing his muscles and oiling his beard? I don't think it would take much to push him over the edge. At the very least, we've got him on drug possession."

Slade nodded. Behind him, Ezra led Ivan away from the booking desk to the interrogation room. His fingers still bit hard into Ivan's arm.

"He's been read his rights?"

Ander nodded. "Said he doesn't want a lawyer. Says he's done nothing and he's got nothing to say to us."

"We'll see about that. We've got drugs, and the gym was Dani and Mac's last known location. That will be enough for a search warrant. I'll get to work on that. As soon as it's through, I want that gym pulled apart." He turned to Stella. "In the meantime, Stella, Hagen, you two can pull *him* apart."

Stella glanced at Hagen.

He nodded.

All of them were ready for some kind of action. They headed straight to the interrogation room. Inside, they found Carlos's partner attaching Ivan's handcuffs to a bar in the middle of the table.

Stella tapped Ezra on the shoulder. "You can take those off."

He frowned. "You sure? He's a big guy and…"

Hagen pulled out a seat and sat down. "We're sure. He might be big and pumped full of 'roids, but there's two of us, which adds to at least four of him. We'll be fine."

Ezra undid the handcuffs and, with one long, lingering glare at Ivan, left the room. The door clanged shut behind him.

Stella took the seat next to Hagen. "Ivan, we've got a whole bunch of questions for you, and we don't have a lot of time, so why don't you—"

"I've got nothing to say." Ivan leaned back in his chair and folded his arms over his tank top. His biceps bulged against his chest.

"Nothing to say, huh? We've got four missing persons, and all of them connected to you."

Ivan shrugged. "So?"

"One of them's your ex-girlfriend's husband."

"You're making me weep."

"The other three are women. You like abducting women, Ivan? Is that your thing?"

Ivan scowled. "Now, just a minute. I'm no kind of—"

Stella planted her hands on the table. "Where's Carlos Guerrero?"

Ivan fell back in the chair. "How the hell would I know?"

Hagen took a deep breath. His jaw was set, his nostrils flared.

Stella swallowed hard. Whatever was burning inside

Hagen was preparing to explode. He'd need to be careful, and she'd need to make sure he stayed careful.

So she did the talking. "Tell me about Veronica Trang."

Ivan rolled his eyes. "The fire inspector? Jeez. She gave me a fine. I paid it and got an electrician to replace some of the wiring. Cost me a damn fortune, but what the hell. It's the price of business. I haven't seen her since she came to the gym and poked her nose in my fuse box."

"What about the two FBI agents who came to your gym today? Where are they?"

"How the hell would I know? They came, they saw, they asked a bunch of dumbass questions, and they left."

Stella blinked. This was getting nowhere. Normally, they'd break him down slowly. They'd wait for him to contradict himself, then chip away at his story until he broke. But they didn't have the time for that. They had to go hard and get straight to the point. But that wasn't working. Frustration rose inside her, an itch that had to be shed, not scratched. They needed to slow down, but everything inside her was yelling *hurry up*.

"Where were you early Friday morning around two o'clock?"

"Two o'clock on Friday morning?" Ivan rubbed his chin. His beard drifted against the back of his hand. "Well, I would've been tucked up in bed with...no, wait. Friday morning? I was at Club Premiere in Nashville. Me and about two hundred other people. That enough witnesses for you?"

He dropped his hand, revealing a smug grin.

If phone records and camera footage confirmed what he said, and she doubted Ivan would have been so specific if he were lying, then he couldn't have abducted Carlos. Not by himself anyway. He was slipping away, leaving them with nothing.

Hagen tapped a finger against the stainless-steel tabletop.

"The pills we found in your gym. You want to tell us who you got them from?"

Ivan shrugged. "Me? I didn't get them from anyone. Don't know what you're talking about."

"They were found in your gym."

"I found a piece of gum under the treadmill the other day. I don't know who put that there either."

Hagen's cheeks burned red, but he kept his voice low and steady.

"You're the only one—the *only one*—with a link to all four of these missing people. You better tell me where they are now, or by God, we'll throw so much crap at you, they'll double the voltage on the electric chair."

Ivan paled and swallowed hard. He looked scared for the first time. "It's a coincidence, man. You've gotta believe me. I don't know what the hell you're talking about. I don't know where Maria's idiot husband is or some fire inspector I met once. And I certainly don't know where your damned FBI agents are. Useless bitches probably got lost on the way home."

A red flash shot across Stella's vision. The worry, the anger, the frustration that had been building all day exploded in a single burst of rage.

She stood, her chair falling out from behind her. She flew across the table, grabbed Ivan by the top of his tank top, and yanked him out of the seat.

In a second, Stella had him bowed over the back of his chair, her eyes boring into his. "You want to watch your mouth," she hissed. "I've got two friends out there, one of them a month away from having a baby, and they're in trouble. You want to leave here in one piece, you'd better start talking."

A hand landed on her arm.

She jerked away.

Hagen grabbed her again, harder this time.

She glared at him.

Concern was written over Hagen's face. "I think we'd better take a break." Stella blinked twice, took a breath, and released her grip on Ivan.

He slumped down into the chair. A small smile flickered under his beard. "You know what? I will take that lawyer now. And I'm entitled to a phone call, too, I believe."

Hagen lowered his chin until he was eye to eye with Ivan. His voice was calm, the words slow and controlled. "We'll make the arrangements."

He placed his hand gently on Stella's lower back and directed her toward the door. She didn't resist. She'd been stupid, out of control. They couldn't afford mistakes like that. Guilt that had burned in her chest and bedded down with anger was exchanged for frustration.

She could kick herself. And Ivan. "I'm sorry, I—"

"It's okay. If you hadn't done that, I would have. Stay here with Chloe and relax. Check his phone. See if he's lying about that nightclub. I'm going to see if Slade has gotten that warrant."

32

Stella slumped into the chair at Carlos Guerrero's desk. She hoped no one could see her. To lose her temper like that, to let emotion overcome her, was embarrassing.

She expected that reaction from Chloe. And from Hagen too. Both of them seemed to have a fire that always burned somewhere deep, just waiting to erupt into mile-high flames at will.

She had always thought that her own inner fire was less likely to explode under pressure.

Mac.

The thought of Mac held somewhere dark and damp, or suffering, fed her flames. Just the idea of her being dropped into a shallow grave made Stella want to tear the whole county apart with her bare hands until she found her.

The station door opened. A figure approached the reception desk. His suit was badly creased, and the halo of graying hair above his ears suggested he'd come either straight from bed or straight from a bar. A battered leather briefcase hung loosely in his hand.

"My name is Winston Brady. I'm here for..." He stepped back and checked his phone. "Ivor Scheffler. I'm his lawyer."

Stella swore quietly.

But...at least the lawyer was so careless that he didn't even know his client's name.

Thanks to the search warrant, they'd have an hour now, maybe two if they were lucky, to find something that would enable them to hold Scheffler for longer and apply some leverage. The gym owner had to know something. He must have something they could use. She could *feel* it. Surely they wouldn't release him while Mac and Dani were still out there.

A deputy led Winston Brady to the interrogation room as Hagen emerged from the security room with Chloe. He threw a small nod in Stella's direction and continued out of the station without stopping.

Chloe joined Stella, perching herself on the edge of Carlos's desk. She held a phone in her hand.

"Hear you blew a gasket in there."

Stella took a deep breath. "Yeah. Sorry, I—"

Chloe grinned. "Good for you, newbie. If you didn't let off steam every now and then, I'd start to think you're half agent, half android. And if you *are* going to let off a jet of steam, a creep like Ivan Scheffler is exactly the place to aim it."

Stella gave her an uneasy smile. Chloe's approval was welcome, even if Stella didn't entirely agree with it.

Chloe waved the phone in her hand. "The sheriff called up Nashville PD to check the creep's alibi, but Slade came through on the search warrant. Hagen and Ander are joining the cops at the gym, seeing if they can find anything else. We've got his phone."

Stella sat up straighter in her chair.

This would usually be Mac's job. She'd plug the phone into a computer, download the data and perform some sort of strange search with software and algorithms and spreadsheets. Someone else would probably do that eventually. They'd sift out the location data and map the call connections. But first, she and Chloe could take a quick look. Maybe something would jump out and send them in a new direction.

Stella took the phone. "We got a password?"

Chloe shook her head. "He seems like a meathead. Try one to six. In order."

Stella plugged in the numbers. "Nope."

"Six zeroes?"

"Seriously?"

Chloe shrugged, giving a small wince as she moved her newly unbraced shoulder. "Our Ivan really doesn't look like a guy with a head for figures. If that doesn't work, I'll go and get his date of birth. After that, we'll have to find a cyber team."

Stella tapped on the screen.

000000.

Apps filled the home page. "Damn."

Stella started with Google and checked his location history. However, for a dumb lug, he'd managed to turn location tracking off.

Chloe dragged a chair around to read over Stella's shoulder. Her breath smelled like menthol.

The messages on the phone seemed to be of little use. Ivan offered bodybuilding advice to friends, praised six-packs, and raised an emoji thumb to flexed pecs. He responded to videos of fights in bars and pictures of muscular women in teeny bikinis. He also appeared to share a number of videos of kittens falling off shelves and sleeping on people's shoulders.

Chloe lifted her eyebrows. "Kittens, huh? I guess no one's

all bad. Maybe we should release him now."

Stella scrolled past the kitty videos. "If we don't find anything better, we might just have to."

A thread appeared to confirm his intention to visit a club in Nashville on the night of Carlos's abduction. Chloe sighed. "Nuts. Try his photos. We might get lucky and find a pic of the place he's holding them."

Though she was starting to believe they'd run into a dead end, Stella brought up the images. Ivan Scheffler might have been the link between all the victims, but beyond that, they had nothing, not even a motive.

None of his messages suggested he was about to do something stupid or cruel. One image after another showed bare-chested men straining to lift weights the size of smart cars or running their fingers over abs that seemed to be made out of cobblestones.

Chloe fell back in her chair and stretched out her legs. "I think this is more your area than mine."

Stella flicked the screen. One near-naked muscleman replaced another, their hips narrow and their thighs mushrooming out of skintight shorts. It was all too much. Too much muscle. Too much flexing and far too much self-regard.

Stella laughed halfheartedly. "A few more pictures like these, and I might just change sides."

Chloe chuckled.

She passed to the next image and stopped. This photo showed the inside of Ivan's gym. At first, it seemed like more of the same. Men with shoulders like bulls squatted and strained in the background. In the foreground, one man heaved himself over the pull-up bar. His eyes were creased with effort, and his thick neck, stretched and red, had veins that looked like they were about to snap.

Stella spread her fingers over the screen, enlarging the

man's face.

There was something familiar about him. A nagging sense she'd seen him somewhere tugged at her gut. Perhaps he'd been in the gym earlier when they'd arrested Ivan. But Stella didn't think so. There'd been a number of men there, all interchangeable, but she couldn't recall this man with his blue eyes and blond hair shaved at the sides.

And yet, she was sure she'd seen him somewhere.

She shook her head. There were more important things to worry about now. She tapped on albums and then tapped again on an album called "The Boys."

The pictures were older. Instead of gym shots and bodybuilders, Ivan's photos showed military tents and men in uniform. These pictures must have been taken before he opened the gym.

In one photo, six men posed in front of an armored Humvee, their M4 carbines hanging from shoulders coated with yellow dust.

The next picture showed three U.S. soldiers working a checkpoint beneath a decaying poster of Saddam Hussein.

In another photo, two women clad in black were captured walking in front of a tattered road sign indicating the distance to Pul-i-Khumri, Baghlan, and almost three hundred kilometers away, Kabul.

Stella flicked on, revealing a pictorial record of Ivan's military service. The images shifted between buddies, bases, and shots taken on patrol. But there was nothing brutal. No closeups of dead jihadis or portraits of frightened, captured enemies. Most of the men in the gallery appeared to be Ivan's closest friends, men who looked like they'd seen action and were glad to have come out of it.

Chloe pulled in her feet and sat up. "Got anything?"

Stella shook her head. "No. At least...I don't think so."

She flicked back to the face that had seemed so familiar.

33

Back at the gym, Hagen stood in Ivan's office with his hands on his hips. Just outside the door, deputies prized open lockers and checked the space above the ceiling tiles. Stationary bikes, punching bags, and barbells sat unused at this point.

A second team, led by the sheriff's department's last handful of deputies, searched Ivan's home. They hadn't found anything yet.

Ander pulled a book off the shelf and studied the cover at arm's length. "*Build a Stronger You*. I'm guessing there's plenty of stuff in here about drinking protein shakes and lifting heavy stuff and nothing at all about finding a steroid dealer and popping pills." He leafed through the pages before dropping the book to the floor and reaching for another.

Hagen crouched in front of the desk and opened the top drawer. "And nothing about kidnapping people either, I'm sure."

Ander held the next book in his hand. He didn't open it. "Tell me something. How sure are you we've got our guy?"

Hagen set a pile of printed material on the desk in front

of the computer monitor and dropped into Ivan's chair. "He's involved. He's got to be. Or knows the person who is. It can't be a coincidence that he's linked to everyone who's gone missing. He's in this. Whether he's in it up to his ankles or his neck, I don't know. But he's not innocent. We just need to find a clue, something that will help us crack him open."

He spread the material he'd found over the surface of the desk. Advertisements for nutritional supplements showed snarling weight lifters hovering over a bottle of little green pills. Pamphlets for self-defense classes displayed men wearing pajama pants delivering unbalanced kicks to coaches covered in padded armor. A number of pamphlets explained what recruits needed to do if they wanted to join the Army, the police, the Marines, or the fire service.

Hagen leafed through them. The pictures of assault courses and men with guns and wraparound shades did little for him. Neither did the call for character, competence, and commitment. The mojo and bragging rights he acquired weren't what had called him to the FBI. He'd joined for many of the same reasons as Stella. To put away the kinds of bad guys who'd killed his father. And to find the one bad guy who did pull the trigger on him. He wanted to be in a position to put that asshole away himself. In a grave, not prison.

Ander placed the book he'd been searching back on the shelf and approached the desk. He shuffled through the pamphlets and the marketing material. "Looks like he's helping guide gym members to the military. Or rather, pulling old military service members into the gym."

Hagen picked out a pamphlet from the fire service and another from the police. "There's a demand for that, I guess. But not just the military. Looks like he specializes in all the uniformed services."

"Services that have seen members go missing. At least one."

"Right." Hagen rolled the top of one of the pamphlets between his fingers. An idea was building in the back of his head, a seed that was already throwing out connections from the gym to the services and the victims.

He pushed a button on the monitor and waited for the screen to boot itself to life. A password field blocked his way.

Ander pointed at the bottom of the monitor. A thin piece of paper had been taped to the edge of the screen. "Try that."

Hagen squinted at the tiny handwriting. He hit the zero key six times, followed by the return key. The screen changed to show an uncomfortably close image of a man's six-pack.

"No genius, is he?"

Ander shrugged. "Maybe he's just got a bad memory."

"You're too generous."

"There. In the corner. The 'membership list' file. Let's see who else comes here."

Hagen clicked on it. The file opened to reveal a list of more than three hundred people who had, at one time or another, joined Ivan's gym.

Ander rocked on his heels. "Bingo. I'd bet you a steak house dinner the person we're looking for is on that list."

"But I'll bet you two steak house dinners and a couple of beers we won't be able to check them all in time. Even if we exclude the people who paid, came once, and never came back."

Ander drummed the top of the desk.

"That's not a bet I'll take. I'm not paying for two steak dinners. Let's hope Stella and Chloe found something better on his phone."

34

The knot on Mac's head from the car crash throbbed. She felt dizzy. Her mouth was dry, and her lips were sore from the duct tape. Her fingertips ached from where he'd held his lighter. At least the spider was long gone, having crawled out her sleeve about thirty minutes earlier.

Relax. Easy now. Fibonacci sequence. One, one, two, three, five...

Slow down. Breathe.

Don't let him see you're afraid. Don't you dare give him that satisfaction!

But there was nothing she could do. Fear was a biological response to danger. Her body trembled, betraying her. Her fingers curled and uncurled, as though that small movement would be enough to release the tape that bound her.

A beefy hand came down and heaved her out of the box as if she were a bag of groceries. The creep held her on his hip with one arm before he dropped her onto a table. Air whooshed out of her nose. He pinned her down with one heavy hand as he taped her to the surface.

And what a table. It tilted so that Mac's head was inches

from the floor and her feet, still bound at the ankles, were five feet in the air. Blood rushed to her head, adding pressure to her wound. She couldn't turn or lift her neck.

Once she was secured, her captor grunted. Satisfied with his work, she supposed. Then he walked away.

The only thing that brought any reassurance was the sight of Dani out of the corner of her eye. But Dani couldn't help her. She was gagged and bound to a chair.

No one could help her.

"Hnnn. Hnnnnn." Dani squirmed. She was no longer looking at Mac. Her gaze was aimed somewhere beyond Mac's feet, at the entrance to the barn.

Thump. Thump. Splosh. Thump. Thump.

Footsteps. The creep's footsteps. She knew that heavy, deliberate tread now. He was back. Quick trip. Her throat tightened. He must have had a bucket of water too. A light splashing of drops hit the barn's earthen floor with every step he took.

What the hell?

The man stopped next to her. To Mac, with her head just below his knees, he appeared to be a giant. He towered over her, his blond hair sitting like a glacier above the shaved sides of his head, his blue eyes staring down from a red, rigid face. A yellow towel was slung over one shoulder, and he was carrying a metal bucket filled with water.

He ripped the duct tape off her mouth. She bit back any sound of pain, though it felt like he tore off three layers of skin.

"What…what are you going…?"

The man placed the bucket on the floor and removed the towel from his shoulder. "What am I going to do? Is that what you're trying to ask?"

"*Hnnn. Hnnnn.*" Dani writhed in her chair again.

Mac's chest tightened.

Dani knew. She knew what he was about to do, and in Dani's wide eyes and growing agitation, Mac could see that it wasn't going to be good.

The man dropped the towel into the bucket and pushed it under the water. "I asked you what you were afraid of, remember?"

Mac tried to nod, but her head was fixed in place by tape that ran over her forehead and under the table.

The man lifted the towel out of the bucket. Water dripped onto the floor. "And you wouldn't tell me. Only name, rank, and serial number. I respect that. Just as you should respect the methods I'm going to use to obtain the information I need. The same methods the government uses."

Then it clicked. He was going to waterboard her.

Before she had time to panic, he folded the sodden towel neatly in two and placed it over her face. She closed her eyes, forcing herself to stay calm.

People didn't die from waterboarding. It only felt like they would.

They survived, and so would she.

She told herself the sensation was refreshing. After the filth of the crate and the humid heat of the barn, the lukewarm water running past her ears, unsticking the dried blood from her skin, was welcome. But she knew what was coming and knew she was lying to herself.

"Hnn. Hnn, hnn."

Mac couldn't see Dani, but her concern sounded stronger, her desperation pitching her muffled cries high and sharp.

A weight, like heavy sand, landed on her face. The water pressure wrapped the towel tightly around her cheeks just before liquid poured into her nostrils. She tried to hold her breath against it, but the shock forced her to inhale. The stream of water came so fast, she couldn't even cough. The towel tightened, gripping her face in a wet vice as though a great, heavy paw had placed itself over her head and wouldn't let go.

The water continued to pour, soaking her face and filling her throat.

The pain, the fear, was greater than anything she'd ever known.

Mac wasn't sure whether she was trying to breathe in or trying to breathe out. Her lungs burned. Her throat was blocked. She was drowning. She thrashed, panicking, against the tape that bound her. Her knuckles beat against the surface of the table, her neck straining against the bindings.

The water stopped, but the pressure stayed, suffocating.

One second.

Two.

Three.

Mac's world dimmed just before the towel was lifted.

She sucked in the fresh air, hot and wet, taking two deep gasps. Relief. Air alone had never felt so good.

The man lowered the bucket. "And now, tell me...what are you afraid of?"

He waited as Mac spit water out of her lungs. She understood. He wasn't trying to drown her. He was trying to frighten her. He wanted to see her beg and cry and tremble with fear.

Screw you. And screw the horse you rode in on.

Mac blinked water away and blew the lukewarm liquid off her lips. It took a couple of coughs and then two big breaths to get enough air. "Don't forget to massage behind my ears next time."

The creep scowled. He lifted the towel from the bucket. Mac took a deep breath just as the fabric covered her face again. When the water began to pour, she was ready.

She hoped.

The sodden cloth gripped her cheeks. Water ran up her nose and settled into the back of her throat again. She had such an urge to cough, to vomit, to shake her head and gasp for breath. Her lungs screamed.

She had to breathe. She had to...

She exhaled and gasped.

As Mac inhaled, the towel was sucked into her open mouth. It brought a flood of water that poured down her throat.

Panic was a living thing sitting on her chest. She couldn't breathe. She would never breathe again. She tried to lift her chin, anything to throw off the flow of water. But the water seemed to come from everywhere. It surrounded her. Swallowed her.

Nooooo!

The water stopped. The towel came off. Mac coughed, and water fountained out of her mouth. After that was over, she desperately filled her lungs with air.

The man lowered the bucket and dropped the towel. He nodded his head slowly, his hands on his hips.

"That's real impressive. Even the best-trained special forces operatives can't resist more than a couple of minutes of waterboarding, but you lasted..." He checked his watch. "You went a whole minute. Better than most. Guess it's not drowning you're afraid of. No more than anyone else, anyhow."

He bent to his ankle and removed a knife from its sheath. The weapon must have been ten inches long, with a curved blade and deep serrations along the back.

"*Hnn. Hnn, hnn.*" Dani squirmed in her chair.

Mac's eyes widened. To have survived waterboarding twice in a row only to be carved like a turkey or dissected like a frog in bio—what a waste.

The man lifted the blade and brought it down just above Mac's ear.

Shhk.

The tape binding Mac's head to the table loosened. She breathed out in relief, the pressure in her aching skull releasing slightly. The man moved down her body. He cut the tape around her midriff and her legs. She slid to the ground with a thud, her already damaged head striking the floor first.

Mac lay on the barn's wet earth. Her hands and ankles were still bound together. She was utterly powerless, able only to scream—though she suspected that, if she tried, she wouldn't be able to do much more than cough.

She certainly couldn't stop the man from coming around the table, hoisting her onto his shoulder, and dropping her into a chair facing Dani.

"Hnn. Hnn."

Dani was holding back tears.

Mac tossed her head. A lock of wet hair was stuck to the side of her face. It didn't move even when she jerked her neck. Pain radiated out from the base of her skull. A trail of water ran down her back, sticking her shirt to her skin.

"I'm okay, Dani." Her words caught in her throat as she spoke. She hadn't noticed she was trembling. She noticed now.

The man ran the tape around her shoulders, pinning Mac to the chair.

Now what?

Whatever he had planned, it couldn't be worse than waterboarding.

She sat straighter, with more confidence. If she could survive that, she could survive anything.

To hell with this lunatic.

Whatever he threw at her now, she could take.

The man squatted in front of her. His face creased into a small half-smile. He reached toward Mac's cheek.

Mac jerked her face away. "Don't touch me, you freak."

"Aw, no reason to be like that." He unpeeled the lock of wet hair from Mac's cheek. "There, that's better, isn't it? See how nice I can be?"

Mac shuddered and yanked her head again. The lock came out of his hand and stuck to her neck.

"What the hell do you want?"

"I told you. I want to know what you're afraid of."

A thousand different curses popped into her head, and she wanted to bellow each one into the lunatic's blond-bristled brain. But it would do no good. The less she said, the better.

"My name is Special Agent Mackenzie Dra—"

"Blah blah blah." The man shrugged. "Well, all right then. You know, I was thinking. Maybe you're afraid of the dark. I can make it dark for you permanently."

He stood up and rummaged in the pocket of his jeans, producing the Zippo he'd used on her fingers earlier. There were blisters on both of her index fingers already.

The silver was tarnished and dented in places, the neck of the engraved eagle on the face of it bent slightly out of shape. He flicked the lid open and closed, open and closed, before opening the lid a final time and sparking the flame.

The blue-and-yellow fire danced above the wick. Its light cast an orange glow in the barn's dark space and sent black shadows dancing over the floor and slipping across the walls. "Let's take a closer look at those pretty eyes, huh?"

"*Hnn. Hnn.*"

The man threw a look at Dani. "No one's talking to you. Shut up."

He turned back to Mac and moved the flame closer to her

face. Mac tensed. She pulled her head back and turned her cheek from the fire.

"Hnn, hnn. Hnnnn."

Click.

The man slammed the lighter closed.

He ripped the tape from Dani's face. "You got something to say?"

Dani's face creased with rage. "Fuck you, you coward! Leave her alone."

The man stepped back. His face paled. "Coward?" He threw the lighter onto the floor and, with a loud crack, delivered a slap to Dani's face that whipped her head sideways and made the chair rock.

"Noooo!" Mac screamed. "Don't touch her. Please. Don't hurt her."

Dani slid her jaw from side to side. A red hand mark spread across her cheek. "I'm okay, Mac. Really. I'm fine. This chickenshit creep can't hurt me."

The man pulled his arm back again. Dani turned her face and braced for the blow.

He lowered his arm slowly. He stared at Dani, looked at Mac, then shifted his gaze from one to the other again. A smile spread across his face.

"Well, now. I guess I can see what you're scared of, little one. And if seeing your friends suffer is what puts the fear in you, I'll be more than happy to oblige."

Horror flooded Mac's heart like water to a bag of cement. "No."

His grin grew wider. "I'll get me two little birds with one big stone."

35

Stella stood in the interrogation room of Pelham Sheriff's Office, gripping the top of the chair. She wished it offered any kind of support. "First, let me just say that I'm very sorry for the way I behaved earlier. I was out of order, and it won't happen again."

Chloe leaned against the door behind her. Stella was sure if Chloe had lost control, she would have preferred to wash down a meal of gravel and glass with a cup of acid than apologize for losing her temper. Especially at a time like this. Especially to a man like Ivan Scheffler.

But the words came out easier than Stella had expected. She had, after all, been out of order. While she would like someone to put Ivan Scheffler against a wall and wipe the smirk off his face, that wasn't her job.

She had a more important job to do. Dani and Mac depended on her.

Ivan's lawyer gave her a small nod of acknowledgment. Stella pulled out the chair and sat down. That lawyer, Brady, was no fool, despite messing up his client's name at first.

Requiring her to apologize before proceeding had given him some leverage, which he was more than happy to pocket.

"Damn right you were out of order." Ivan folded his arms. "I'm gonna write to my congressman. That's what I'm gonna do. Next security job you'll have, lady, will be crossing guard at a primary school."

Chloe snorted.

Stella relaxed. She leaned back in her chair. "You do that, Ivan. I'm sure your congressman will be very interested to hear from you."

Ivan lifted a finger and started to speak.

Brady interrupted him. "Now that that's all settled, how about releasing my client, and we'll say no more about it?"

Stella placed Ivan's phone on the table. "I'm hoping your client will say a little more actually. Because that big bag of steroids and methamphetamine we found in his gym is speaking volumes. And I reckon a jury will have a lot to say about it too. Possession with the intent to distribute and sell." She rubbed her pointer finger and thumb together. "That's big money and jail time."

Ivan rubbed the back of his hand against his beard. "I don't know nothing about that."

Brady intervened. "What jury, Agent? What are we talking about? A Class D felony? Doesn't the FBI have anything better to do?"

Chloe pushed herself away from the wall and placed both hands on the surface of the table. "Class C and D felonies with a minimum fifty thousand-dollar fine attached. There's a lot that we should be doing. And he's going to help us do it."

"Now, Agent, there's no need—"

"Fifty thousand dollars?" Ivan's face paled. His jaw opened. He leaned toward his lawyer and spoke quietly. "What's she talking about?"

Brady tapped his client's arm. "Don't worry. I'm sure it won't—"

"We just need a little help, that's all." Stella opened Ivan's phone. "You're right, Mr. Brady. We have bigger fish to fry. We need your client to identify some people for us."

Ivan glanced at his lawyer.

He responded with the kind of small, silent nod that had the power to kick an investigation wide open.

Stella picked up the phone and opened the photo app. A bare-chested man with pecs as hard and flat as cutting boards lifted a barbell. She turned the phone toward Ivan. "Who's that guy?"

Ivan pulled the phone closer. "That's Kevin. You want his number, Agent? Is that what this is all about? You only had to ask. Though, frankly, I gotta tell you, you're not really his type. He likes them with a bit more…" Ivan cupped his chest. A leer spread across his face.

His lawyer seemed to find something particularly interesting under his own fingernails while all this was going on.

Stella chewed on the inside of her cheek. Shutting down this guy's gym was starting to look more attractive by the minute. She flicked the screen. The next picture showed a man pulling at a rowing machine, the muscles on his back forming a pile of smooth, symmetrical hillocks. "And this guy?"

"That's Barry. 'Bear,' we call him. What's going on, Agent? Planning a party?"

Stella ignored him. She flicked through a couple more images until she found the picture of the blond man heaving himself over the pull-up bar. "And who's this guy?"

Ivan's face paled. He sat back in the chair and shrugged. "Just a guy at the gym."

Stella glanced at Chloe. She licked her lips.

She feels it too. There's something here.

Stella held out the photo of the blond man's face. "Fifty thousand dollars, Ivan. How long did it take you to build that gym? You want to throw all that work away for this guy?"

Brady stopped fussing with his fingernails. "I think we're done here—"

"You might have fifty grand you can throw away. But I don't." Ivan shook his head at his lawyer. "I put my life in that gym. Wolf. That's Wolf."

Stella frowned. The nickname meant nothing to her. She still couldn't place where she'd seen him. "Who's Wolf?"

Ivan shrugged. "He's just a guy. That's all."

Stella gritted her teeth. Frustration was starting to eat at her again. Rage flamed somewhere behind her eyes.

Easy now. Don't give him any more help than you already have.

She took the phone again and opened the contacts list. She scrolled down the page. One man's name followed another. A long line of Aarons, Abes, and Andrews gave way to Barrys, Bens, and Brads.

If there was a woman's name in that list, it was well hidden.

Stella scrolled until she came to names starting with W. There was a Walter, a Warren, and a couple of Wills.

And there it was. Wolf.

Chloe reached past Stella's shoulder and took the phone. She hit the dial button and put the phone on speaker. The phone rang once, twice, three times before a voice answered.

"Hey, Ivan. Listen, I'm in the middle of something here. What's up?"

There was something strange in Ivan's expression. A concern. Fear. Almost a plea for mercy. He said nothing.

The voice came again. "Ivan, we must have a bad connection. Hey, look, I'm going to have to turn the phone off for a while, but I'll call you later, man. Okay?"

The line disconnected.

Stella leaned across the table until her forehead almost touched Ivan's nose. "Who the hell was that?"

Ivan swallowed again. The color returned to his face. He folded his arms and locked his eyes on Stella.

He's decided. He's not going to help.

Dammit!

Chloe glanced at Stella. "Let's just see who that number's registered to."

Ivan smirked. "Like that's going to help you. Dude uses burners like he's…the Unabomber or something. I have to switch out his contact number more often than…than I change my underwear." Ivan seemed awfully proud of his impromptu joke. "Starting to think he's onto something, though. Government all up in my business."

Stella clenched her jaw. If Wolf was using a burner and he'd turned it off, the number they had was mostly useless. In the best-case scenario, it would take a day or two to get the phone provider to turn over info. A day or two may as well be infinity for Dani and Mac.

The door opened. Hagen strode in. His naturally lean form contrasted sharply with Ivan's inflated frame. This was a man who was comfortable with who he was, who didn't feel he needed to model himself on anyone's idea of how a man should appear. It was enough for him to dress the way he wanted and to stay in shape. Hagen didn't need more than that.

His appearance refreshed Stella's own confidence like a splash of water to the face.

Together, we'll beat this guy. Together, we'll find Mac and Dani, and we'll find them in time.

Hagen laid a pile of pages on the table. Ivan glanced at the top sheet and scowled. Hagen ignored him.

"How we doing here?"

Chloe lifted her chin. "Ivan was just wondering whether he should tell us who this Wolf guy is or pay a fifty thousand-dollar fine for being a drug-dealing cretin."

"Hey!" Ivan slammed his palms on the table.

Brady gripped his client's upper arm and whispered in his ear.

Hagen licked the tip of his finger and leafed through the pages. "'Wolf,' you say. Here you are. No surname but there is a phone number. I guess you've checked it already?"

Stella nodded toward Ivan. "He says it's a burner. We haven't looked yet, but I doubt even he's dumb enough to lie about that."

Ivan scowled. "Hey!"

Hagen lifted an eyebrow. "You trying to tell us you *are* dumb enough to lie about that? Ivan, I really don't think you can be dumber than we think you are."

Stella twisted her ear stud. Ivan sat at the center of this whole thing, like a node on a web connecting all the victims. If he wasn't involved, someone close to him was.

And judging by Ivan's reaction, Wolf was a pretty good candidate.

If only she could remember why this Wolf character felt familiar.

Hagen gave Stella a quick wink and turned back to Ivan. "Okay, here's what we're going to do. This is a list of all your members, current and past. We've also got your contact list. We'll haul in everyone you know. Everyone who so much as sniffed the sweat in your gym will get a visit from a couple of deputies who will grill them about what they saw, what they heard, and what drugs you supplied them with. By the time we're done, I suspect a fine will be the stuff of dreams. Your gym? That will be gone."

Hagen folded his hands on the table. "But we can make that all go away, Ivan. Help us now, and we'll overlook the bag of Arnolds we confiscated. You don't know who they belong to. We don't know who they belong to. We keep the pills. You keep your gym. How does that sound to you?"

Ivan rubbed his hand over his beard but said nothing.

Brady whispered to Ivan, leaning into his ear.

Ivan nodded.

His lawyer broke his silence. "My client will cooperate. We'll want it in writing."

Hagen flipped through the pages on the table and retrieved two stapled sheets. Stella smiled. He'd prepared everything.

The lawyer read the first page, moved on to the second, and gave Ivan a nod.

Ivan signed. "So what do you want to know?"

Stella tapped the phone screen again. Her finger bounced on Wolf's face. "Who's this guy?"

Ivan scratched his cheek. "I told you. He's just a guy at the gym. He's just Wolf. That's what we call him."

"Real name?"

"Waylon. Waylon Gray. But no one calls him that. He likes to be called Wolf, and we like to pretend it suits him."

Stella frowned. Waylon Gray. The name meant nothing to her. "What do you mean, you pretend the name suits him?"

"He's just kind of, I dunno. I...I sorta feel sorry for him."

"You feel sorry for Waylon Gray? Why? Who is he?"

"He's just a guy. Ex-military, if that's what you want to know. Kinda."

Hagen lifted an eyebrow. "Kinda?"

Ivan fell back in his chair. He looked like a dog rolling onto his back and baring his stomach. "Yeah. He was military, but not for long. He got through basic and was sent straight to Iraq. He went out on his first patrol the day after he landed. I don't know what happened exactly. He says there was a big battle. He was hurt and invalided out, and he says the Army washed its hands of him."

Stella frowned. "Right. And what do *you* think happened?"

"I don't know. I just heard, that's all."

"Heard what, Ivan?"

Ivan sighed again. "Okay, okay. But you didn't hear it from me. He's not a bad kid. He's just a bit…you know. Not all there. What I heard was that he was in the third Humvee in a convoy. After the first one hit an IED and was blown halfway into orbit, the other two came under fire. And Wolf…what I heard was he ran away. He just…jumped, turned on his heels, and bolted. Left his friends under fire. He reappeared at the base two days later, spinning some story about escaping from the Mahdi Army or something. The Army had him back home and out of uniform before he even got the sand out of his boots. You can't do shit like that."

Stella tugged at her ear, the stud spinning freely. "I'm surprised you'd let a guy like that into your gym. Your place doesn't look very welcoming for people who left their brothers behind."

Ivan pulled his immunity agreement closer to his lawyer. "Shows what you know, Agent. That whole place is a foxhole. Half the guys there have had one kind of trouble or another. Wolf? He's like any number of guys who thought they were G.I. Joe, reached the battlefield, and then found out they couldn't cut it. He's not a bad guy, but he lives in a fantasy world. I felt kinda sorry for him—"

"You said that already," Stella interrupted.

"Yeah, well, he's been rejected from every government job he's applied for. Fire service, sheriff's office, you name it."

In an instant, the room seemed to stretch. Ivan and his

lawyer seemed far away, as if they'd suddenly been sucked down a long hallway.

Ivan's words echoed in her brain.

Rejected from every government job he's applied for. Fire service, sheriff's office...you name it.

Ivan didn't notice Stella's reaction. But in that instant, she saw right through him. He didn't have compassion for this guy, he was terrified of him.

Ivan ran a hand over his flattop. "Yeah, the gym's been good for him. Gives him a new purpose, you know?"

Hagen snorted. "If you like the guy so much, why do you seem scared of him?"

Of course, Hagen saw it too.

"Look, I'm not scared."

"You seem scared. You've been protecting him for no good reason."

"I keep my eye on him. Like all the other guys, he's got history. He's...*sensitive* to a lot of things. He stays late a lot. He lives alone and gets lonely out there on his farm in the evenings. So sometimes we get a drink after a workout. He was good to talk to when I broke up with Maria and when that fire inspector you've been banging on about dropped that fine on me. We drank those bitches off together."

Stella's eyes widened. There it was.

All that separated them from Mac and Dani was the space between this room and Wolf's hideout.

She leaned forward, nudging Hagen out of the way. "Where is he?" Stella had to hold herself back from diving across the table and grabbing Ivan by the shirt again. "Where does Waylon Gray live?"

Ivan shrugged. "No idea. Some farm near Pelham somewhere."

Stella yanked out her phone. She opened a map and searched for Pelham. "Where? Show me where."

"I don't know. I've never been there." Ivan pulled the map closer and made a circle over the screen with his finger. "He said he's close to Montgomery Avenue, so I guess he must be somewhere around here."

Stella turned the phone around and showed the screen to Hagen and Chloe. Wolf was in the area they'd just searched.

36

Hagen grabbed Ivan's phone and strode out of the interrogation room. He heard Stella and Chloe scramble to catch up. Chairs scraped against the tile floor. "We've got to narrow this down, and we've got to do it now."

He ignored Ivan shouting through the door. "Hey, what about me?"

A deputy walked toward Hagen with his neck bent over a sheet of paper.

Hagen stopped in front of him. "Hey, who's in charge of technology around here?"

The officer lifted his head. He jerked a thumb over his shoulder. "Try Jeffers."

Hagen stepped around the deputy and followed the line of his thumb. Another deputy sat at a desk, scowling through glasses at a monitor.

"You Jeffers?"

The deputy peered over the top of his glasses. "Yeah, how can I—?"

"I need a fix on a phone number."

He scrolled through the contacts. Stella and Chloe joined him. "Wolf's practically the last one."

Chloe peeled away. "I'll go get Slade and then start on a background check." She set off down the corridor to the station's security room.

Hagen's thumb stopped moving. He showed the phone to Jeffers. "Here."

Jeffers typed the number into the computer. He shook his head. "I'm getting nothing. Show me again."

He retyped the number. Once more, the screen told them that none of the computing power of the sheriff's office, the FBI, and the combined capacity of law enforcement could produce a location for Wolf's phone.

A small, hot explosion fired in Hagen's chest.

Damn! It must be the rural area.

He pulled the phone back and pushed the number.

"You have reached..." The robotic voice rattled off the phone number.

Hagen shook his head. "There's no connection. He definitely turned off his phone."

The air seemed to have leaked out of Stella, and yet as she lifted her head, Hagen was sure he could almost see a flame burning behind those dark eyes. They had a lead. For the first time since Mac and Dani had disappeared, they had a solid lead. And Stella had landed it.

"What have you got?"

Slade's deep voice sounded behind him. Hagen turned to find him and Chloe. His boss's face was like stone, his eyes focused entirely on Hagen.

"It looks like we've got him. A member of Ivan's gym. Ex-military. Ivan told him about Maria and about Veronica. And he's been turned down by the sheriff's office and the fire service."

Stella's eyes widened. "And the FBI. *That's* where I know

him. I saw him at the office during that recruitment day. And I saw him again. Yesterday morning. He was walking away from the building just as I came in. He'd removed his cap and shirt. Just had a tight, white t-shirt on. He must've shoved them in his bag."

Hagen jumped in. "That must've been just after he put the note on the door."

Chloe took a deep breath. "And I saw him on recruitment day! I held the damn door for him, and we exchanged goodbyes. Well, I said good luck as he sized me up. Pretty clear what you're afraid of now, boss. Same thing we're all afraid of."

Slade's expression didn't change. "We're not losing anyone." His voice lowered to a growl. "Where is he?"

Hagen shook his head. "That's what we're trying to find out. His phone's off, and Ivan doesn't have the address. His record keeping is shoddy as hell. We can try to ping his last location but that'll take a while. All we've got is an area of farmland near Pelham, which we've already checked."

"And his application." Stella was vibrating with energy. "He applied here, at the sheriff's office. They'll have his application. His name is Waylon Gray."

Slade nodded, already prepared with a plan of action. "Get out to the grid around the crash site. I'll dig up his application and send you the exact location. Just get the hell out there. Go!"

Stella and Hagen shot like cannonballs out the office door.

Chloe trailed behind, catching up next to Stella. "He was after me, Stella. Not them. He sized me up like a rabid dog would a bone. He was practically salivating."

"Chloe." Hagen didn't have the words or the time to mend the chink in this tough agent's armor. "C'mon, let's save our friends."

37

To think this all started with a note.
No...not just a note. A memorandum.
A killer memo if ever one had been written.

Now, here we were. The special agents sat opposite each other. Wasn't more than six feet between them. They could've had a good old chat if they weren't both gagged again. But I wanted them to be able to see each other, see the pain and fear exchanged from one set of eyes to the other.

I didn't want them talking to each other, supporting each other. They could have built up each other's courage. I didn't want them to do that. This mission was about fear and overcoming it on your own.

Nice and natural. That was what I wanted. A natural reaction.

As I hurt one, the other would be forced to sit there and watch. No way to avoid it. I hung a light on the post so they could see each other better. The glare put one side of their faces in shadow and made the other side white and bright, but each could see the other suffer well enough.

They'd have a true test of courage. It was time.

I stood between them and put my hands on my hips. "Now, which one of you is the bravest, huh?"

They stared at me, both of them.

I expected them to protest or something, try to speak. But they just watched me like I was speaking Swahili. Mac was still wet and dripping, her hair clinging to the side of her face. And the other one, Agent Jameson, just looked like she was going to burst into tears, like she was on the edge of enough. I'd be lying if I said that wasn't a satisfying sight.

I spoke slowly, like I was addressing the *hard of understanding*. "I'll give you a bit of help. How about that? The answer is neither of you. The bravest person here is me. *Me*! I'm the bravest. I *am*. I can look death in the face and laugh. I can stare down anything the world can throw at me. I'm braver than all of you, braver than the sheriff's office, the fire service, and the *damned* FBI combined. I'll show you all."

My voice rose as I spoke. By the end, I was shouting. My fingers trembled, and my eyes teared from lack of sleep. I didn't want them to see that. I turned my back on them and strode into the shadows near the wall.

Calm down. Don't let them see what you're feeling. Think of something that makes you happy. The muscle ache that comes after a workout. A cold beverage on a summer evening. A beer with the guys.

The guys.

I remembered them. Philly and Dutch and Steve-o. Last time I saw them, we were piling out of that Humvee on the outskirts of Kut. I couldn't tell one from the other in their camo. The team was like one tangle of camouflage tripping over itself. They clawed at the ground, trying to get purchase.

The first vehicle was in flames, a big column of black smoke rising into the sky. The smell of burning rubber and gunpowder...and flesh. I thought it was flesh, burning my nostrils.

And the crackling. I thought it was the fire at first. The sound was like dry wood in a fireplace. But then came whistling and the sharper thud of the bullets hitting the stones and the sand around us. The thud of the RPG hitting the ground and the boom of the second rocket hitting the other Humvee.

I didn't look. I just ran. There was a crater about twenty yards away on the other side of the road. I didn't know what created it. An older explosion, I guess. An old IED. I dove into it and put my head down.

No one joined me. The guys didn't come like I thought they would. But the crackling grew louder. And the screams. They were so loud. So desperate. Like I could do something about them. Like they expected me to run back and do something.

But I wasn't a medic. I couldn't make it stop. There was nothing I could do to help them. I just lay there in that hole with my face buried in the sand and my hands over my ears until, eventually, when darkness fell, I crawled away. I kept going. I wasn't afraid to die. I just couldn't do anything.

That was what I told myself, what I told the commanding officer, and what I told everyone at the base. But they didn't believe me.

They all thought I was a coward, that I didn't have the courage to be a soldier. Said I ran from that fight. And the Army, they put it on my record. Dishonorable discharge. A black mark that followed me everywhere I went.

Now I was going to show them how wrong they were. *They* were the cowards, not me.

I held out my hands in the darkness. My fingers only trembled a little now. Excitement, that's what it was. Anticipation. Nothing to do with fear.

Reaching down to my calf, I pulled my knife out of its sheath. Had a good blade, that knife. Almost ten inches long, with a curved edge and a serrated back like the teeth of a crocodile. So far, it hadn't cut anything tougher than duct tape, and I didn't even need a knife for that.

That blade was going to be christened with blood now, a lot of it. No getting around that. Can't cut into someone's flesh without spilling a river.

The thought made my mouth dry.

There they were, the pair of them, sitting in that little puddle of yellowish light shining from the hanging bulb. I couldn't see them too clearly. They were mostly just silhouettes.

Mac barely even made a shape in the chair. That's how small she was. Anyone looking at that seat could have thought they were just looking at a chair with a couple of thin cushions.

I chuckled.

Their faces turned toward me, but they couldn't see me, not in those shadows. Just not enough light in the corner where I stood, my blade in my hand.

But the other one, Agent Jameson. There was no mistaking her. She was taller than Mac, and the bulge in her belly was so big and round, it was like she was sitting with a basketball on her lap.

Easiest thing in the world to sink a knife into.

I shuddered. I didn't mean to, but I did.

Nothing could be scarier than that. Just the thought of the agent being cut would send her into a screaming fit, even through her gag. And Mac? Surely she wouldn't have the courage to just sit there and watch something like that happen to a friend.

They'd break in a second. Both of them.

I swallowed.

I'd have to stab a pregnant woman in the belly with a ten-inch blade. I'd done some things in my time, but this was a whole new world. They always said stabbing was a very personal way to kill.

Time to get personal.

There was no coming back from stabbing a pregnant woman. That's the sort of thing that would change you forever.

The handle of the knife grew damp with sweat.

Get a grip on yourself, soldier. Show them who you are!

I grasped the knife tighter. It felt good and heavy in my hand. Strong. Unbending. That's what I needed to be. Like a knife. Sharp. Unstoppable.

I strode back to the light. When they saw me, the two of them started squirming in their seats like I'd set fire to their chair legs or something.

"*Hnnn. Hnnn!*"

Never been gladder that I'd gagged them again.

I stood there under the light and willed my hand to stop shaking.

You can do this. Don't be frightened now. It's just a little blood. You've killed two already. What's a couple more to your total?

My gaze dropped to the agent's belly.

Or three.

Agent Jameson's eyes were pleading. Tears ran down her cheeks and rolled over the duct tape in streams.

Mac's eyes? They were fiery. If she could have gotten out of that chair, I was pretty sure she would have scratched my face off with her bare fingers.

"All right, listen up. Here's what's going to happen."

I turned from one to the other. They were listening to me, or at least hearing me. I had their attention anyhow.

"I'm going to kill one of you. I'm going to do it real slow. I'm not gonna lie. It will hurt, and things are going to get real messy."

"*Hnnn. Hnnn!*"

That was Mac this time. She rocked in her chair and pulled at the tape. The tops of her cheeks were as red as the dried blood that still stained her shirt.

Agent Jameson didn't make a sound. She just lowered her head and let the tears drip onto her belly. Her shoulders sagged, and I...I felt sorry for her.

The thought of what I was about to do made me feel like I'd swallowed an artillery shell whole. The weight sat deep inside me, waiting to tear me apart.

Be brave, soldier! Complete the mission. Then you can rest.

"This one." I waved the knife over Agent Jameson. "This is the one I'm going to kill. And you, Mac, are going to sit there and watch."

Mac shook in her chair so hard, I thought she might tear that thing apart.

"Now, now, Mac. Agent Jameson sealed her fate when she kicked me in the face. You can still live. All you have to do is face your fear. Watch and don't react."

Agent Jameson just sobbed and sobbed, like she had a whole sea inside her, and the only way it was coming out was through her eyes.

I crouched down in front of Jameson and waved my blade.

Mac tried to shout louder. *"HRRG. HRRGH. HRRRGG!"* The cries came from deep in her chest.

I froze.

It took me back, that noise. Dragged me to a place I didn't want to go.

While I was lying there in that crater, a couple of the Mahdi Army had turned up. They didn't see me, but I saw them well enough. They walked up to one of the soldiers who had been in the second Humvee. I didn't even know his name yet. He was just about to be rotated home. He'd been hit when he'd gotten out of the Humvee, but he was alive, all right.

I didn't know what they did to him. I couldn't look. But I heard him. He just made that deep, guttural noise until he stopped and made no more noise at all.

That was when I crawled away.

My breath came faster. Sweat pooled in my palm again. I almost dropped my knife.

I couldn't do it. I just…couldn't.

"Dammit!"

I stood up and walked away from them, back into the darkness.

I needed support, the help of a buddy. I reached for my phone.

38

Stella closed the Velcro on her bulletproof vest and jammed her back against the back seat of the vehicle. Her spine ached, and her muscles were sore, but the adrenaline spiraling through her system blocked the pain.

They were the second vehicle in a three-vehicle convoy of black Explorers. Pelham County deputies had taken over the driving duties because they knew the landscape better. Ezra Forman, Guerrero's partner, was behind the wheel.

Hagen, who'd taken shotgun, spoke to Ezra. "Slade will call in a sec to confirm that the address and coordinates he sent is our target. It's about five minutes out. A small farmhouse behind a small copse of trees. Hard to see from the road."

"Roger that."

Five minutes out felt too long to Stella. They had to find them now. They *had* to rescue them.

SWAT was scrambled, but the closest team was still half an hour behind them.

Chloe was squeezed between Stella and Ander in the back of the Explorer. Stella could practically hear the voice in her head pleading to a higher power. *Please be alive to rescue.*

"What do we know about this place?" Chloe squeaked out the question.

A burst of classical music rang from Hagen's phone. He took the call. "Let's find out. Boss?"

Slade's voice filled the van. "It's confirmed. We got the address from his FBI application and cross-checked it with his police and fire service details. They match. It's a small place, less than fifty acres. It's in his grandparent's name, but a deeper dive shows that Waylon Gray inherited it six years ago but left it derelict while he was in the Army. He came back to it after he was discharged for going AWOL when his unit was ambushed in Iraq."

Stella leaned closer to the SUV's microphone. "Do we know what happened there?"

"I've just read the report. The patrol hit an IED. Waylon was the only one uninjured, but the Mahdi Army was on the scene in seconds. They finished off anyone who was left alive while Waylon hid in a crater nearby. It was two days before he turned up at the base again. He was dishonorably discharged, barely avoiding a court martial." Slade paused. "Listen, I'm on my way. Be careful there."

The phone went dead.

Chloe lowered her head. "We should've searched this place first."

Stella shook her head. "Someone did, or at least reported that it'd been checked. We can't be everywhere at once."

"No time for regrets or pointing fingers. Let's make sure we're ready." Hagen returned his phone to his pocket and pulled out his Glock. He checked the magazine and shoved the rounds back into his weapon.

Stella swallowed. There was a pretty good chance the Glock was how this was going to go down. Unless Waylon

Gray, the man Ivan knew as Wolf, came out with his hands up and screaming for mercy, he wasn't going to have a good night.

Chloe broke the silence. "Why do you think he does this? The kidnappings?"

Hagen re-holstered his gun. "He's a nut. There's no why."

"He might've been trying to help his friend." Stella folded her hands between her legs. She was aware of the gun on her hip, but she wasn't going to touch it. Not yet. Not unless she needed to.

Over the past few weeks, she'd been in several confrontations with armed madmen. A couple of situations wound up with the bad guys shooting first. She'd watch and focus tonight. No hesitation if she determined the situation warranted deadly action. Dani and Mac depended on her.

Stella connected the dots for the team as she saw it. "Ivan told Wolf about Maria and about the fire inspector. When he wanted to get back at the government organizations that rejected him because of his discharge, they were good places to begin. Easy targets."

"You think he hunted Trang down like he was tracking an animal? All the way to Rugz Textiles?" Chloe wondered.

Hagen ventured a theory. "Collins is ex-military. That's a small world. I bet he's buddies with Waylon Gray too."

"I bet Collins is a member at Ivan's gym. Or an ex-member who let himself go," Stella added.

"That's an understatement." Hagen shook his head.

"And Dani and Mac?" Chloe sounded like she was savoring the names of their friends, giving them the respect they deserved.

Stella shook her head. "Bad luck, I guess. They came into the gym to talk to Ivan about Maria. Our guy was there working out and saw two FBI agents bugging that same friend. Like a spider seeing two juicy flies blunder into his web."

Ander glanced over at her. "Weren't you two planning to go to the gym? Until Dani had other ideas?"

Stella's mouth turned to cotton. Ander was right. If her mother hadn't called, she and Chloe would have gone to the gym instead of Mac and Dani. They could have been the ones abducted, and Mac and Dani would have been sitting in the SUV, hoping they were still alive.

Ander patted her arm. "That's how luck works. Good for some, bad for others. And now you get to even things up."

Stella didn't reply.

The convoy sped on. Outside, the new moon's sliver kept the fields in darkness. They became blacker and blacker as they grew closer to their target.

Hagen turned in his seat. "When we get there, we'll—"

The theme song to *Rocky* blasted out from someone's phone.

Stella sat up straight. *Rocky?* None of them had that ringtone.

Hagen fished in his pocket and retrieved Ivan's phone. He glanced at the others.

Stella nodded, answering his silent question.

Hagen pushed the button and turned on the speaker. Wolf's voice sounded through the vehicle. "Ivan? Hey, listen, man. I need some help. I've got this thing, and I...it's hard, man. I just need you to tell me I can do it. Like you do in the gym. Tell me that hard things need hard men like you always do. Tell me I can do it."

No one spoke. Stella strained to make out background noise. There was nothing. No other voices, neither Mac's nor Dani's.

"Ivan? Come on, man."

"Wolf?" Hagen pitched his voice a little deeper to imitate Ivan.

It took everything Stella had not to scream at him.

"Ivan? *Come on*! Are you there?"

"Here."

Stella knew he was keeping his sentences as short as he could so Wolf couldn't catch the vocal difference. But knowing the strategy didn't lower her frustration.

"Are you driving? I hear—"

The phone went dead. Wolf had hung up.

"Shit." Chloe tightened her vest again.

Hagen banged on the window of the vehicle and shouted to Ezra. "Move, move, move. Let's go!"

Ezra didn't need to be told twice. He radioed the lead SUV. Every driver hit the gas.

The convoy raced down the road. Hagen held Ivan's phone so tight his knuckles were pale.

Stella could practically feel him willing Wolf to call back. But Wolf knew something was wrong now. She figured he had to.

Stella stared at the dark screen. Was he putting it all together?

Was he on the run, aware that if he stuck around, he would soon be caught or killed?

Or was he trying to finish his mission while he still had the chance?

But maybe that call meant that Mac and Dani *were* still alive. Maybe killing them was the difficult thing he was struggling to do.

Or maybe he had already killed them, and he needed Ivan's encouragement to dispose of their bodies.

Stella shook her head.

Don't think like that. You can't think like that. They're alive, and we're going to keep them that way.

The driver shouted from the front seat. "Two minutes."

In two minutes, she'd be with Mac again. She'd lead her out of there and get her home safe and sound. Stella set her jaw.

Mac is not your friend. Dani is not your friend. They're victims. Abductees. You're a professional, and you're going to do your best to save them because that is what you do. That's your job.

Distance. Professionalism. Expertise. That's what she needed now. It was always possible that they could fail. Mac and Dani could already be dead. She needed to be prepared for that.

No. Stella couldn't lose someone again. She couldn't. The thought of going back down that hole sent a shiver down her spine. Better to be cold and unmoving than shattered and broken.

Ezra spoke over his shoulder, his voice quiet and low. "We're here."

39

The Explorer slowed, then stopped. The vehicles in front and behind did the same, their lights off. Ander pushed open the back door and dropped out, his weapon in his hand. Stella followed. They stood in front of a small copse of elms and poplars.

Through the trees, Stella could make out the shape of a small house, a blacker form against the darkness of the night. To the right of the house stood an older model truck. On the left, a low building shaped like a barn skulked in the shadows of a tree.

No one spoke. A night breeze rustled the branches and set the leaves whispering. Their noise hid the soft sounds of Hagen's footsteps as he slipped through the woods to meet the sheriff's deputies. He signaled they should take the house and the truck, then snuck quietly back to the team.

"We'll take the barn."

Stella nodded. Wolf was more likely to do his dirty work in a barn than in his home.

They reached the end of the copse.

Stella crouched behind the trunk of a poplar tree. Chloe

and Ander spread out along the edge of the woods. In front of them, the house was dark. The barn didn't appear to have any windows.

Hagen lifted a hand and jabbed a finger forward three times.

In the darkness, two figures raced silently toward the house. One stopped next to the front window. The other stopped next to the door. Two more figures ran around the back. The deputies were in position.

A yellow light flashed, illuminating the truck's bed, and extinguished on finding it empty.

Hagen jabbed his finger again.

Go!

Stella raced toward the barn. Her feet pounded against the soil. She kept her footing steady, taking care not to trip on tree roots. Her weapon was in her hand, though she had no memory of drawing it.

Ander and Hagen's heavier footsteps thumped behind her, and after them came the softer sounds of Chloe moving off to Stella's left.

Stella's right foot caught on a rise in the ground. She stumbled, her knee striking the ground. She was up again in an instant.

From behind her, a beam from a flashlight lit up two long bulges, like waves carved into the ground, each about the length of a person.

Two graves.

Four missing people.

Stella's heart thumped in her chest. Two people were dead. And two people were still alive. There was still some hope.

Maybe.

She ran harder.

A thin sliver of yellow light leaked through the barn

where the door met the wall. She sprinted on, stopping only when she reached the door handle. Hagen slipped behind her, and Chloe took the opposite side of the door. To Stella's right, Ander crouched, his gun trained on the barn's opening.

Hagen's hand dropped on Stella's shoulder.

She turned the handle and pulled open the door. Slowly. Quietly. When she could see into the space inside, she stopped.

A light hung from the side of a pillar. A dirty glow fell on two chairs that faced each other, about six feet apart.

Dani. Mac.

There they were. They were alive or appeared to be alive. Both of them sat straight in the chairs.

Dani faced the barn door. Her feet were taped to the chair legs, her face puffy and damp. Her red hair tangled around her face. But she was alive.

Stella couldn't see Mac's face, but she was alive too.

And they seemed to be alone.

As Stella shifted the door open, Dani glanced over. Just her eyes moved.

Mac had her back to the door, and her arms were bound behind her, but she twisted her shoulders when Dani's focus shifted and looked to the side. Stella stood in the doorway but kept back in the shadows.

"Hnn. Hnnnn." Dani tried to speak.

Stella took a step into the barn, lifting a hand. *It's okay. We're here. You're safe.* She didn't say the words but willed the women to understand her from the look in her eyes.

Dani's eyes opened wider, shaking her head.

Stella slowed. Stopped.

From the shadows behind Dani, a figure emerged. He was big, well over six feet, with shoulders as wide as a bull. In one hand, he gripped a large knife. He seemed to grow in the light.

That was the man she'd passed in the parking garage.

As Stella's fingers curled around the handle of her gun, he dropped into a squat, using Dani as a shield. All Stella saw was the left side of his face and the silver blade of his knife resting under Dani's chin.

Dammit.

A tear ran down Dani's face. The agent had never seemed so vulnerable. She'd always been so strong and supportive, a pillar in the office. She held everyone up even when they were at their most down.

Stella just wanted to dart forward and hug her, assure her that everything would be fine.

She stepped forward, lowering the muzzle of her weapon. "Waylon? Or should I call you Wolf?"

"Wolf." His voice was a growl. "Call me Wolf."

"Okay. Wolf. We've met, right?"

Behind Stella, Hagen slipped to the left along the wall of the barn while Ander moved to the right. Stella sensed, even without looking behind her, Chloe on her right shoulder, her gun outstretched.

Wolf snarled. "Remember me, huh?"

"Sure. You came in for recruitment day, didn't you? And I saw you when I came to the office yesterday. When you left the note on the door."

Wolf grinned. "Is he scared, your boss? Slade? Is he quaking in his boots now?"

Stella spread her feet, keeping her weight balanced. "Sure. He's worried. He's spent the last few hours in the control room, overseeing the search for our colleagues."

"Very brave. Hiding in a control room. Why didn't he come out himself if he's so tough?"

"We all play our roles. I've seen Slade rush into a scene to save a wounded teammate." Beside her, Chloe shifted. "Because that's what we do, right? Go into scary situations and get the job done. That's what you wanted to do, right? Get the job done. It's why you wanted to be one of us, Wolf."

The big man's grin melted. "But you didn't want me, did you? Not the FBI or the fire service or the damn sheriff's office. You said I couldn't cut it, that I wasn't brave enough. Now I'll show you just what you're missing."

He moved the blade closer to Dani's throat.

Dani whimpered.

On Stella's left, Hagen shifted. He was looking for an angle, trying to find a line of fire.

"Stop!" Wolf wrapped an arm around Dani's forehead and exposed more of her neck to his knife. "One more move, and I'll open her right up."

Stella stretched an arm toward Hagen, willing him not to move. "Is that what you wanted to show us, Wolf? That you can kill people?"

Wolf opened his fingers, gripping the hilt of his knife between his thumb and his palm. One by one, he returned each finger to the handle. "Oh, I've already shown you that. Those two mounds out there by the wall? They're all the proof you need that I have the guts to kill when I need to."

A shudder passed through Stella. She hoped Wolf didn't notice.

"You bastard." Chloe stepped into Stella's peripheral vision. "If you kill Dani or Mac, if you so much as scratch Dani's neck, I swear to God, I'll—"

"So," Stella interrupted. "What *did* you want to show us, Wolf?"

"What do you think I wanted to show you? My courage, of course." His voice had risen to a roar. "*My courage*! They said I was a coward. They said I was scared. A chicken. Well, I've shown them. I've shown you. Look at what I've done. Abducted a sheriff's deputy. Kidnapped a fire inspector. And I killed them both. And then I took two FBI agents. Two! Do you see? I'm willing to step into tough situations too. How brave am I now? You see?"

Stella shook her head. "No. I really don't. There's nothing brave about killing someone, Wolf. Anyone can do that. And plenty have. And there's nothing courageous about dying for nothing either. Listen to me, Wolf." She took a terrible gamble and lowered her gun entirely. "I know what happened over there in Iraq. I gotta tell you, I would've done the same thing. We all would have."

Wolf blinked. He didn't speak.

Stella licked her lips and pushed on. "Courage isn't killing, Wolf. Courage is the ability to feel fear and do the scary thing anyway. It's having the guts to do the right thing when the wrong thing is *so* much easier. It's what lets you try even though you think you'll fail. And when you do fail, it powers you to get up and try again."

Wolf still didn't move. Stella couldn't tell what he was thinking, but she seemed to be getting through. She was almost sure she was.

Just a little more.

She looked at Mac and Dani. She glanced at Hagen to her left, at Chloe on her right, and found the figure of Ander in the shadows near the wall.

"Courage, Wolf, is drawing close to someone even though you know you might lose them." She stared Wolf straight in the eye. "The brave thing to do now, Wolf, the hard thing to do, is to drop the knife and take responsibility for what you've done. Courage means putting down the knife and coming with us. Are you brave enough to do that?"

Wolf licked his lips. His blade moved against Dani's throat. A tear spilled onto her cheek but was absorbed by a strip of red hair that was stuck to her face.

Stella stepped forward again. She stood right behind Mac.

"Show me how brave you can be, Wolf."

In the bulb's bare light, a tear glinted on Wolf's cheek.

Stella took a step.

Wolf didn't react.

Stella took another step and another. She passed Mac, her right hand brushing her friend's damp shoulder. Relief at Mac's survival deepened and solidified. She had touched her, felt her. She *was* alive.

She stood in front of Dani. Their eyes met. There was no panic in Dani's gaze. The tears that welled above her cheeks showed fear and worry, but the way Dani held her eye contact displayed mostly defiance and resilience.

Stella gave her a small nod. Then she trained her eyes on Wolf.

"Face the thing you're most afraid of. You can do it." She took the back of Wolf's hand and pulled the knife away from Dani's neck, removing the blade from his grip.

Wolf stood up, and she tossed the weapon away. He might have been more than six feet tall, but in that barn, he seemed smaller than Mac. He dropped his head onto Stella's shoulder and sobbed like a frightened child.

40

"Here you go, Stella. And the juice is on the house."

Kate, the server at Coco's, slid a plate and a large glass of orange juice onto Stella's sidewalk table. The plate was loaded with Stella's favorite Sunday brunch.

A couple of fried eggs nestled against some hash browns that rubbed against a bowl of fruit salad, two triangles of toast, and a small dish of smashed avocado. Soft piano music sounded through the café's speakers, giving the day the quiet start it deserved.

Stella pulled the plate closer. "Thanks, Kate. What's with the juice? Not that I don't appreciate it, but…"

Kate shrugged. "I guessed you needed it. Vitamin C. Good for your immune system. Rough night, huh?"

Stella pulled her ponytail over her shoulder. Apparently, she looked as exhausted as she felt. She sighed. "Something like that."

"Hey, we've all been there. If we didn't have Saturday night, we wouldn't need Sunday morning." Kate grinned. "I'll fetch your cocoa. Can't start your day without that."

As Kate headed back to the kitchen, Stella lifted her fork

and stabbed her egg. The yolk emptied its yellow blood into the bottom of the hash browns.

Rough night was an understatement. Stella and the team had left the deputies to take Wolf into custody and seal off the scene around the farmhouse. The sheriff's office would have a lot of work to do today. There were two bodies to exhume. Marlowe had driven out to the homes of Maria Guerrero and Phil Trang to break the news.

Stella didn't envy the sheriff. To add to it, she felt guilty for how grateful she was that she didn't have to recover from the death of her friend. Just the thought brought a bulge to the back of her throat.

She chewed on a forkful of yolk-soaked hash browns as Kate left her cocoa on the table.

The rest of the night flashed by in a moment.

Slade had turned up—the siren on his Expedition screaming—at about the same time as the ambulances.

He had told Stella to ride with Mac and sent Chloe with Dani while he stayed in the barn and examined the crime scene. Apart from those orders, he barely spoke more than two words. Then the paramedics slammed the doors.

Stella sat next to Mac, holding her hand all the way to the hospital.

Except for the occasional utterance of a sequence of numbers, Mac was mostly silent on the drive, her bubbly personality popped and flat. Stella didn't ask. She knew it had to be a coping mechanism. The blood on the side of Mac's head had long since congealed into a black mess, staining her white-blond hair. It was like she'd been to war.

Stella stayed until the nurse gave her friend a sedative, until her head sank into the pillow and her eyes drifted closed.

Mac was still at the hospital in the room next to Dani.

The pair of them would stay for a day or two more, for tests and observation. Dani might be there even longer.

Sleep would probably help Mac most.

A shower, some good food, and a dirty martini would probably do even more good down the road.

Stella hadn't reached home before three and hadn't fallen asleep much before five. For two hours, she'd tossed and turned, appalled at how close she'd come to losing a friend. But that she had someone whose loss could move her so much also brought her a deep sense of belonging.

That was a new and strange feeling. She hadn't felt like this since before her father had died, when they were all a family.

Stella took a long draught of orange juice. Kate was onto something. Fresh juice was a pretty good way to recover from a rough Saturday night.

Maybe she should make OJ her new favorite drink and lay off the cocoa. She shook her head. She really was exhausted.

She finished the eggs and hash browns. The morning was already almost gone, and she wanted to get back to the hospital. Slade was probably already there, and it would be her last chance to see Dani before she went on maternity leave.

Stella's phone vibrated on the table, making ripples in her orange juice and clashing with the gentle notes of the café's piano music. Stella tilted the screen toward her.

Hagen. On a Sunday.

Stella's thumb hovered over the green button.

The case was done, and anything else related to the FBI could wait until Monday. Either he was just calling to see how she was, to chat and shoot the breeze like a good friend. Or he was calling to talk about Joel.

Both possibilities knotted her stomach.

She took the call. "Hey, Hagen."

Silence. Hagen's reply took a second too long. He felt unsure about everything too.

"Stella. You at home? Or you back at the hospital already?"

Stella reached for her cocoa. Its warmth was deeply comforting. "Getting brunch. And then I'll head to the hospital. See how Mac's doing. And Dani."

"Right…right."

The line fell silent again.

They both broke the silence at the same time. "Listen."

They laughed.

Hagen's laughter ended first. "Go ahead."

"Uh-uh. You called me. What did you want to say?"

Silence again.

"Erm…listen. I need to talk to you. There's something I have to tell you. I should've told you the other night before… you know, this whole new case came up, but I can't wait anymore. You need to know. I'll come over now before you go to the hospital. I'll be over in about ten minutes."

Stella frowned. "Hey, look—"

Beep-beep.

Another call. *Shoot.*

"Just a second, Hagen."

Stella shook her head as she clicked over.

Slade's deep voice sounded in her ear. "Stella? Grab your stuff and head over to Kentwood. We've got a body. Three of them. And it's another weird one."

The End
To be continued…

Thank you for reading.
All of the *Stella Knox Series* books can be found on Amazon.

ACKNOWLEDGMENTS

How does one properly thank everyone involved in taking a dream and making it a reality? Here goes.

In addition to our families, whose unending support provided the foundation for us to find the time and energy to put these thoughts on paper, we want to thank the editors who polished our words and made them shine.

Many thanks to our publisher for risking taking on two newbies and giving us the confidence to become bona fide authors.

More than anyone, we want to thank you, our readers, for sharing your most important asset, your time, with this book. We hope with all our hearts we made it worthwhile.

Much love,

Mary & Stacy

ABOUT THE AUTHOR

Mary Stone

Mary Stone lives among the majestic Blue Ridge Mountains of East Tennessee with her two dogs, four cats, a couple of energetic boys, and a very patient husband.

As a young girl, she would go to bed every night, wondering what type of creature might be lurking underneath. It wasn't until she was older that she learned that the creatures she needed to most fear were human.

Today, she creates vivid stories with courageous, strong heroines and dastardly villains. She invites you to enter her world of serial killers, FBI agents but never damsels in distress. Her female characters can handle themselves, going toe-to-toe with any male character, protagonist or antagonist.

Discover more about Mary Stone on her website.
www.authormarystone.com

Stacy O'Hare

Growing up in West Virginia, most of the women in Stacy O'Hare's family worked in the medical field. Stacy was no exception and followed in their footsteps, becoming a nurse's aid. It wasn't until she had a comatose patient she became attached to and made up a whole life story about—with a past as an FBI agent included—that she discovered her love of stories. She started jotting them down, and typing them out, and expanding them when she got off shift. Somehow, they turned into a book. Then another. Now, she's over the moon to be releasing her first series.

Connect with Mary Online

facebook.com/authormarystone
goodreads.com/AuthorMaryStone
bookbub.com/profile/3378576590
pinterest.com/MaryStoneAuthor

Made in United States
North Haven, CT
09 October 2022